# THE SCROLLS OF DESTINY

## THE LAST TEMPLARS - BOOK 3

### PRESTON WILLIAM CHILD

# BOOKS BY PRESTON WILLIAM CHILD

All Books by Preston William Child in Order

http://prestonwilliamchild.com/books

# PROLOGUE

Retired Navy Captain Augustus Tucker Baird shivered under the large, black umbrella loaned to him by the funeral parlor for protection from the cold rain while he said his final goodbye at the graveside of his beloved wife, Eleanor. He pulled his raincoat tight at the neck with his free hand to keep the chilly, early morning air at bay. The wind brought the low, rumbling sound of thunder from somewhere far off.

Despite the deep, soulful sadness he felt for having lost the love of his life, a small smile formed on his face when he thought of how perfect she would have thought the setting to be. A cool, gentle rain and soft, rolling thunder always made her happy. And that was exactly what she had as she was lowered into the ground that first day of spring.

"I just love listening to it!" Eleanor had told him when it

began to rain on their first date nearly 50 years before. "I always have. But now more than ever, it makes me feel so alive to hear it while I'm warm and comfortable and enjoying being here with you."

Father Patterson, the rector for Saint Paul's Church, spoke of his fondest memories of Eleanor at her grave-side on that bracing Alexandria, Virginia morning. As he prepared to leave, he gave the captain a card with his mobile phone number on it.

"Call me anytime, day or night, if you need to talk," he said softly as he shook the stoic Navy veteran's hand.

"I'll do that, Father," Baird said softly, unsure that he meant it, and quickly tucked the card away. "Thank you for being here. Eleanor thought the world of you, and I'm grateful for your help in doing this the way I know she would want it."

"Someday, perhaps over lunch, you can tell me how on earth you procured this site so close to The Grave of the Female Stranger," the rector said with a smile. "I know Eleanor was a hopeless romantic. And though, like the rest of us, she knew little about 'the lady,' she once told me she would never tire of hearing the love story of how 'the lady' was laid to rest here two centuries ago by her husband, who obviously loved her deeply."

"It was the least I could do, Father," the captain said. "My Eleanor motivated every good decision I ever made. I miss her terribly already. But someday we'll be together again."

"Perhaps we can talk about that over lunch sometime as well," the rector said and departed with another handshake.

Shortly afterward, Captain Baird climbed into the back of the limo that waited to take him home. On the way, he relived memories of the day he and Eleanor met, the day they married, and the day she helped him decide to make the Navy a career. That thought resurrected others of how three years earlier, her quick intervention prevented a severe bout of depression from tragically ending his highly decorated career.

The captain still had no clue how a phantom-like Black Operation somehow swept aboard the nuclear aircraft carrier USS Ronald Reagan unseen and prevented his turning it over to the People's Republic of China. But that event led to his treatment and a full recovery, which saved him from the destruction and humiliation that surely would have resulted from his madness.

The aging seadog harbored a boatload of gratitude for the life he was able to enjoy following that incredible but unheralded, top-secret operation. Thanks to whoever the unknown participants were, he'd spent the last two years of his beloved Eleanor's life caring for her while she bravely battled cancer—instead of languishing in prison, just when she needed him most.

As he stepped into the solitude of his now-too-quiet home, the dashing, silver-haired captain hoped for the thousandth time that someday he would learn the facts regarding that fateful day in the Sea of Japan and be able to personally thank those who rescued him from his demons.

# INTRODUCTION

That first day of spring, the morning air was cold on Montana's Flathead Lake. Ice still clung to some stretches of shoreline as John "Doc" Holiday rowed his racing shell as hard and fast as he could. The 26-foot carbon-fiber beauty silently sliced through the glimmering, glass-like surface of the water in the first light of day. About three miles from where he put in, the former Navy SEAL and Secret Service Special Agent was sweating heavily and stopped the craft long enough to shed his hoodie and tie it loosely around his waist.

Before gripping the oars again, Doc took in the serene wonder of the vast lake and the mountains that cradle it. He loved the solace of the early morning. Being on the water at sunrise calmed and refreshed him like nothing else could. Daybreak cast the mountain ridges all around him in silhouette, and the stars were still bright in the blue-black sky. The air and water were so still he could hear two Mourning Doves calling on shore.

After several slow, deep breaths of fresh morning air, Doc began rowing again. He started slow, then picked up speed for one last sprint across the water. Just as he again hit maximum speed, the encrypted satellite phone strapped to his backpack in the stern, his direct link to President Donald Prescott began to vibrate, and the presidential seal filled the screen.

"Damn it!" Doc whispered to himself, and for the first time ever, he ignored the call.

The noble but weary soldier of fortune knew President Prescott would call again in a few minutes, and Doc needed the time to ready himself for the conversation he guessed was to come. During their last conversation a month earlier, he'd told the president he felt he was nearing the end of his usefulness to the nation. Over the past two years, Doc and his elite operations team had fearlessly and very successfully completed several ultra-secret missions at the request of the president. Each was vital to national security. But the latest mission lasted weeks and was the most dangerous. It exacted heavy physical and emotional tolls on Doc, his team members, and their spouses. Doc and his crew hunted down Jonah Baird, a genius billionaire aerospace mogul who had gone mad and began calling himself "the Keeper." Now Baird led an army of henchmen he called "Guardians" who murdered famous authors and artists around the globe. They initially staged the murders to look like suicides, but soon gave up the charade and just blatantly killed.

Baird snuffed out his victims because their creative works offended his twisted mind for one reason or another…or for no reason at all. It was Doc who uncovered Baird's "Forbidden Library," an underground bunker, where the mad genius grotesquely displayed his victims' offending works beside mementos of their murders. Even more terrifying, the modern-day monster had tried to retrieve two undetonated nuclear bombs rumored to have somehow been lost by the U.S. military during the Cold War. The homicidal maniac planned to threaten the U.S. and other nations with the devices unless they handed over millions of dollars, which he planned to use to help finance his global campaign of death.

The hunt was an exhausting, deadly adventure in which Doc and his band of shadow warriors battled Baird's legion of Guardians from the southern coast of Georgia to the treacherous and deadly cold Bering Strait. Greatly outnumbered at every turn, Doc and his warriors fearlessly ran headlong into the breach armed with some of the most-exotic, high-tech weapons known (and unknown) to man. When Doc and his team engineered Baird's capture, the surviving Guardians were either imprisoned or scattered in the wind.

But that's not the end of the story. It's just the beginning. Baird proved to be a formidable escape artist. After his second escape, Doc had had enough of the hunt. But the president didn't have that luxury, which is why Doc's satellite phone began to vibrate again.

"Good morning, Mr. President," Doc said as cheerfully as he could. "What a surprise!"

# 1

## DEATH IN THE WIND

D oc had the oars of his shell in hand and was about to head toward home when he saw Q, the U.S. Marshal on his team, approaching in the small motorboat Doc kept tied up at the dock.

"Good morning, Q," Doc said with a sigh as he lowered the oars into the water.

"Well, don't you look like your dog just got run over?" Q said flatly. "I can understand that 'cause it's colder than a well-digger's ass out here. But how come you look so overheated?"

"I just spoke with the president," Doc replied with a grimace and rubbed his head.

"Don't tell me," Q shot back. "Jonah Baird's broke out of prison again. Right?"

"No, he's still locked up," Doc answered. "But believe it or not, that's the problem."

"How in the world can that be a problem?" Q asked cynically.

"Well, as usual, I'm sure the president is holding some info back," Doc said. "But apparently Secretary of State MacDonnaly painted him into a tight corner late last night when talking with French President DuPris and overcommitted before checking with the boss."

"So far, it sounds like a bureaucratic governmental problem, which we make a point of never getting involved in," Q said dismissively.

"Yeah, except this one could potentially involve Jonah Baird, which could open a whole new can of worms for the nation—and God only knows how many other nations," Doc told him.

"Just tell me what's going on, Doc," Q said with exasperation. "I'm a big boy."

"France has a rogue national hero who's apparently had some kind of psychological breakdown and vanished for months, then turned up in Arizona. Before going public with the news, the French government wants to be sure they understand what's going on," Doc explained.

"The French have a hero?" Q feigned surprise.

"Do you want to hear this or don't you?" Doc asked impatiently.

"Sorry," Q said with almost-believable sincerity.

"The subject is a former member of France's RPMI

special forces. For the past three years, he's served as a highly decorated member of an elite French Foreign Legion strike force based somewhere in the Andaman Islands in the Bay of Bengal," Doc said.

"The middle of nowhere," Q noted.

"Yeah, but yesterday French GIGN special forces military police arrested the mystery man near Sedona, and Secretary MacDonnaly agreed to hold him at Gitmo until France figures out what he might be up to and whether others are involved," Doc explained.

"What's to figure out?" Q asked flatly. "The guy's a loon…end of story."

"The Legionnaire is a national icon. Last year, he was awarded France's Legion of Honor for singlehandedly foiling a plot to assassinate DuPris. Now the French people think he's the Lone Ranger, G.I. Joe, and Superman all rolled into one,

"Kinda like you and me," Q could not resist saying.

Doc ignored the comment and continued his story.

"He went AWOL and popped up near Sedona just prior to our last visit to the White House two months ago. The FBI had him on their radar, and they told the president he had said he'd read about Baird and wanted to be his 'partner.' But he seemed harmless enough until a couple of days ago when the DGSE—France's counterpart to our CIA—stumbled onto some notes he left behind in France, in which he laid out a plan of his own to kill DuPris. The FBI and DGSE took him into custody yesterday. And last night, MacDonnaly agreed to hold him at Gitmo, shackled 24/7 in solitary confinement, under watch by GIGN military police."

"He was plotting to kill the man whose life he saved a year ago?" Q asked incredulously. "That makes absolutely no sense!"

"I'm glad you're paying attention," Doc said with a wry smile.

"I am," Q shot back. "And I still don't see why any of this should involve us."

"Jonah Baird's locked up in Gitmo too," Doc answered.

"Since when?!" Q almost shouted.

"Since the second time he escaped, and the president finally got tired of it."

"Okay," Q huffed. "Baird's locked down in solitary confinement and the French Rambo is in shackles with his own personal jailers around the clock. Sounds like everything's under control to me. So I still don't understand why the president called you."

"You're not going to like the answer," Doc warned him.

"Try me," Q said and braced himself.

"Do you remember our last trip to the White House?" Doc asked. "Remember how the President called me before we even made it back to our hotels, and he told me Baird had escaped for the first time?"

"How could I forget?" Q answered as he gripped a gunwale on Doc's shell to keep the boats together and got comfortable for what he guessed would be an unpleasant story.

"The president told me then that he was deeply concerned because two weeks earlier our intelligence folks had advised him they had a mentally unstable, AWOL French Foreign Legionnaire under surveillance in central Arizona, not far from the federal prison where Baird was being held. The Frenchman had told an informant he was really Nostradamus, and he had a plan to help Baird escape.

"Well, that crazy Frenchman is now in lockdown at Gitmo along with Baird. So the president's concerned the Nostradamus wannabe might put his escape plan into action and take Baird with him. But the French have made it clear the loony Mr. Nostradamus is *their* responsibility, and they won't allow U.S. involvement in handling him. So the president has agreed to a 'hands-off' posture for now. But he wants the comfort of having us standing by in case things spin out of control."

"It sounds like politics to me, Doc," Q said. "And we don't get involved in politics, right? Please tell me that hasn't changed, Doc."

"Q, we both know that everything we do can potentially involve politics," Doc said. "National security drives our missions. But there's always a danger that politics could climb into a passenger seat. That's one of the reasons why we operate in secret."

"Which brings me to my other big concern," Q shot back. "Lately, it seems more and more like we operate with less and less secrecy. The Guardians knew way too much about our movements during the last mission. It's a miracle we all came out of it alive...our wives especially. Madeleine insists on being involved, and Jenny's a hardcore Marine, but Marsha and Connie are another matter. They're keeping up a brave front. But I just can't keep putting them in danger. *I just can't!*"

"Take it easy, partner," Doc said softly. "I hear what you're saying, and I couldn't agree more. Those two have the hearts of lionesses, but they're not wired for our line of work. The truth is, we never guessed what it would take to bring Baird to justice. How could we? He's a genius, for Christ's sake. And thanks to us he became a billionaire...and then he lost his mind! We helped create a monster, and he threw more at us than anyone had ever bargained for."

"He's still throwing it at us, Doc!" Q raised his voice. "He'll keep throwing it as long as we're in the hunt. And what exactly is in it for us? We have more money than we'll ever be able to spend. And I've just about reached the point where all I want is one full day in a rocking chair. Look around you, Doc. We're in heaven! We're rich and sharin' it all with the loves of our lives. We've conquered the world...but Baird, or the Keeper, or whatever the hell he calls himself *this week* still haunts us. It's time to let it go!"

"Whoa, Q!" Doc said as he opened his arms wide and tried one more time to calm his friend down. "Get some perspective. The truth is, Baird made all this possible. So there was a blessing in the midst of the curse. I hear what you're saying, and I agree with almost all of it. But I can't let go just yet. I'll understand if you and the others walk away. But I'm partly responsible for the evil Baird unleashed on the world. And I can't rest until I know that he can never unleash it again."

"So you're sayin' you're in this for Baird, and Baird only?" Q asked.

"For Baird and Baird only," Doc confirmed.

"And the president knows that?" Q pressed for certainty.

"That's what I told him," Doc said sincerely.

"Well then, I'm in it with you, partner," Q said cautiously. "*And I swear if he breaks out one more time, I'll blow him to kingdom come!*"

"Get a grip, Q," Doc still tried to calm his friend. "You're wound-up tight as an over-wound pocket watch."

"Lay off me, Doc," Q shot back. "I'm cool as a cucumber."

Doc was about to argue the point when their conversation was interrupted by a low, growling sound rapidly closing in from a distance.

"What's that sound?" Q asked as he scanned the sky and water around them.

"Sounds like a drone," Doc replied as he too scanned the surroundings.

That's when they saw it. A black drone about 18 inches across zoomed by, flying east to west about 20 feet in the air, at about 30 miles an hour. The duo watched it as it circled around for another fly-by.

"Who in blazes is flyin' a drone at 6:30 in the morning?" Q asked in complete irritation.

"Probably some kid who can't sleep," Doc guessed.

"I don't think so. Not clear out here," Q countered. "Not hovering around us like this. It could be a Guardian surveilling us."

"Take it easy, Q," Doc tried to reason with his friend one more time.

Q stood up in the motorboat and threw back a tarp to reveal a 12-gauge Benelli M2 XRail shotgun.

"What did you bring that out here for?!" Doc practically shouted at Q.

"You can never be too careful, Amigo," Q replied.

"Please tell me you don't have all 24 rounds loaded into that, Q," Doc said plaintively.

Q did not respond as he picked the weapon up and aimed it at the drone.

"Cover your ears, cowboy!" Q warned Doc as he squeezed the X-Rail's trigger, and it erupted with a roar.

The #4 lead shot disintegrated the drone into a cloud of smoke and pulverized plastic that rained down on the men and their boats as the roar of the gun blast echoed around them.

"Q, you're acting like an idiot!" Doc snapped at his friend.

"That was no innocent drone," Q shot back. "Take a look around you, Doc. We're at least a half mile from shore. Do you really believe some kid had a sophisticated enough drone to fly it out here and hover it directly over us? Someone was making sure it was us."

"You're getting paranoid, Q," Doc said dismissively.

Before Q could answer, four more drones arrived and circled above the men in a tightening formation about ten feet in the air. Q raised the X-Rail again, but Doc bolted from the shell to the motorboat and yanked the barrel of the shotgun downward.

"Don't shoot, Q!" Doc shouted as he pushed the start button, and the motorboat's outboard motor came alive.

Doc tightly gripped a towline from the shell and wildly whipped the steering wheel of the motorboat, sending Q and the shotgun to the floor. The bow of the boat rose out of the water as Doc raced it in zigzags and tight loops, changing direction constantly.

"Have you lost your mind?!" Q shouted as he rolled about on the floor of the motorboat.

Doc suddenly powered the boat in a straight line, and the drones fell into formation, single file, two feet apart, and chased the boat with explosives attached.

"Shoot them, Q! Shoot them now!" Doc shouted and held the boat on course.

Q squeezed the trigger of the X-Rail and sent a shower of lead shot off the stern over Doc's head, spraying the drones, which exploded one by one with a roar and mild concussion. The boat ran aground on the shore seconds after the last drone exploded, and the duo rolled out onto the sand with sixteen shells left in the X-Rail. The morning was suddenly silent again.

"Still think a kid was at the controls of those things?" Q asked Doc sarcastically.

"Looks like the Guardians have been reactivated with brand new toys," Doc replied.

The pair sprawled in the sand, tight beside the motorboat, and scanned the lakeshore for any sign of a threat. They saw nothing unusual. Their assailant was either on the far side of the lake or on the water somewhere much closer. Doc drew his Wilson Combat X9 1911 pistol from his ankle holster and felt a deep need to use it. But their deadly enemy was invisible that Montana morning.

The brothers in arms were alone, except for the birds in the air and the waves washing ashore. The danger had passed close by and was gone as suddenly as it had appeared.

"I'm done running from these rats!" Q bolted to his feet and shouted. "I mean it! I'm done! I won't quit until every last one of them is locked up or buried."

"That's two of us, partner!" Doc said and joined Q on his feet. "Death's in the wind again."

Q laid the X-Rail across his right shoulder, and Doc set the safety on his 1911 and held it close to his leg as they cautiously headed up the hill toward the lake house.

"You know they know the house," Q said to his friend.

"Yeah, I know," Doc said. "But I think they were just yanking our chain to let us know their back. The question is: Why?"

"They scattered when Baird went to prison. And they'd only reactivate if they expected Baird to be on the loose again soon," Q said with certainty.

"I believe you're right," Doc said and spun around to ensure the coast was still clear. "It looks like they intend to take us out of the equation to clear the way for Baird to get back to work on his so-called Forbidden Library."

"Then it looks like you and President Prescott are right about this Nostradamus guy," Q said with a shake of his head. "He's got to be nuttier than a fruitcake to travel halfway around the world to join forces with Baird…but for what purpose? What's his role in all this?"

"I don't know," Doc said as he led the way into the lake house. "But I *do know* we were wrong to think we had defeated Baird. We simply won the opening battle of an evil world war. Now the next battle has begun. And I swear this battle *will* end the war once and for all. When we win it, I hope we'll understand all this. But all I understand right now is that the only way to end this is to put Baird in his grave."

Doc strode across the living room and moved a picture hanging on the wall beside the fireplace, which released a pull-down ladder that was concealed in a recess in the ceiling. He bounded up the ladder, used a block and tackle to lower a large metal chest to the living room floor, then bounded back down and opened the chest. Inside, was a cache of assault weapons Q never dreamed Doc had accumulated.

"Give me a hand with these, Q," he said as he lifted a blanket and uncovered three MAHEMs, nestled among a number of other exotic weapons.

Half assault rifle, half rocket-propelled bomb, the MAHEM is a deadly weapon that weighs as much as a bazooka but is far more accurate and much easier to operate.

"Whoa, partner!" Q said softly. "What are these monsters?"

"Hydrodynamic Explosive Munitions," Doc said with a slight chuckle.

"But their friends just call them MAHEM. They generate an electromagnetic field to produce a molten metal projectile that can penetrate up to ten inches of armor plating and blow a 30-inch hole in block walls up to 18 inches thick."

Doc quickly assembled two of the weapons and handed one to Q to acquaint him with its weight and balance.

"Are you sure this can inflict that much damage?" Q asked his friend.

"It did all that and more in my SEAL days," Doc assured him as he leaned both weapons against the wall beside the front door. "If any suspicious vehicles show up, we're going to blow them clear to hell...*then* call 9-1-1."

"It's going to wake the neighbors," Q said sardonically.

"I'm willing to risk it," Doc laughed. "But I'll bet we'll have a much harder time explaining it to our wives."

Doc retracted the ladder back into the ceiling to avoid the predictable questions when Connie awoke. Then he slipped on his hooded, roper-length sheepskin coat.

"Give me a hand moving this chest to the porch, Q," Doc requested.

"This weighs a ton, Doc," Q grunted as he hefted his end of the chest. "What all have you got in here?"

"Some things you've seen and a few you haven't," Doc replied cryptically.

The duo got comfortable in high-back rockers on the front porch, rested their MAHEMs in their laps, and put their feet up on the chest. Doc pulled his 9mm 1911 nine-shot from his shoulder holster and checked the clip to make sure it was full. Q slipped his right hand under his down coat and rested it on his Browning Hi-Power Mark III 9mm with its 20-shot clip. He enjoyed the assurance of its presence in his thigh holster. If Guardians showed themselves, the duo was ready for them

# 2

# NOSTRADAMUS AND THE KEEPER

Solitary confinement at the U.S. Guantanamo Bay Detention Camp is dark and cramped and silent. Detainees can go insane from sensory deprivation in that concrete void. By the time the French prisoner known only as Nostradamus was introduced to "the hole," the Keeper had already befriended it. The absence of distraction sharpened the Keeper's focus on making his next escape. He was so focused, in fact, the guards had all lost the "Scream Pool" they'd created when the Keeper first arrived. The longest guess —30 days—had come and gone, and still, his cell was as silent when it held him as when it was empty.

As happened every Wednesday at precisely 2:50 p.m., the two-inch by eight-inch hatch in the cell door squeaked open, and a blade of light from the guard's flashlight mercilessly collided with the Keeper's optic nerves.

"Time for your 'Weekly,' Keeper!" the guard shouted. "Move your ass!"

The Keeper jumped to his feet the moment he heard the hatch slide open. It signaled the start of the hour he was out of the cell each week. As three guards stood like statues in the doorway of his windowless five-feet by eight-feet cell, he assumed the "X" position against the back wall. He spread his legs wide, so the outsides of his feet touched the side walls. Then he extended his arms up and out and placed his palms flat against the walls just below shackles that hung from lag bolts anchored into the 18-inch-thick concrete. Only then did the guards enter the cell. The lead guard carried shackles. The other two followed and flanked him with their pistols trained on Jonah Baird, the prisoner they knew only as "the Keeper." Baird's identity was kept secret to help ensure other detainees did not find out he was wealthy. That could create too many challenges for all concerned.

The transport maneuver never varied. The lead guard dropped the shackles to the floor at Baird's feet long enough to close the wall-mounted shackles around his wrists. The iron bracelets held Baird stone-still from the waist up. Then he put his feet together, and the guard attached shackles to his ankles. Once Baird's legs were shackled, the guard released his wrists from the wall shackles and replaced them one at a time with the transport shackles. Baird then waddled out of the cell and began the quarter-mile trek to the showers surrounded by the silent trio of armed guards.

During each trip to the shower, Baird counted the 1,507 steps in his head. The ritual had become part of his obsession of learning every inch of Gitmo he could. He stepped inside the circle painted on the shower floor and braced himself for the welcome hot, soapy water that pummeled his parched, sweaty body for exactly three and a half minutes. The power of the water disintegrated the sweat-stained paper tunic he wore. When the shower ended, he stood naked with his arms and legs spread out, engulfed in a 30-second blast of warm air that dried him. Then the lead guard slipped another paper tunic over Baird's head, and the trio led him along the 983 steps to his weekly 45 minutes with Dr. Thomas Cooper, "the Gitmo Shrink." Baird's shackles were locked into lag bolts in the legs and top of a metal table that was anchored to the cement floor in the center of Dr. Cooper's office. The guards then stepped out of the office, and Baird hung his shaved head.

"How are you this week, Jonah?" Dr. Cooper asked as he sat across the table and began Baird's weekly battery of questions.

As always, Baird said nothing.

"How are the guards treating you?" Dr. Cooper asked.

Baird said nothing.

"Is the food satisfactory?" Dr. Cooper asked.

Baird said nothing.

"Do you have any physical or emotional complaints?" the doctor asked.

Baird said nothing.

"Do you know how long you've been here?" the doctor asked.

But still, Baird said nothing.

"What can I do to persuade you to talk with me, Jonah?" the doctor asked with a sigh.

Dr. Cooper felt personal compassion for Baird and sincerely wanted to help him achieve any emotional healing possible. So during this particular visit, he extended himself beyond the medical protocol and tried to reach his patient on a more personal level.

"Jonah, I understand from your profile and history given to me when you arrived that you lost your wife nearly three years ago. I've read between the lines of that information, and I understand that you enjoyed an immensely fulfilling marriage. I also understand that the two of you were unable to have children, and you did not adopt because your career required an inordinate amount of time and travel. Nevertheless, it appears that the two of you enjoyed the sort of bond most couples can only wish for. I am sorry for your loss of that relationship.

"Then shortly thereafter, your brother suffered a nervous breakdown that abruptly ended his Naval career. It's not unusual for familial traumas of such magnitude to overwhelm someone. I've no doubt they contributed to your ending up here. I want to help you explore and understand these and the other forces that caused you to fall from the top of the economic and industrial worlds to join us on this God-forsaken island.

"You seemingly had it all, Jonah," the psychiatrist said. "The media called you 'a modern-day Edison, whose future seems limitless.' You've been awarded more than two hundred important chemical and mechanical patents. Less than two decades ago, you founded and led Dark Yonder, the multi-billion-dollar global powerhouse in the aerospace industry, competing with SpaceX and Blue Origin for space exploration contracts that will shape the future of the world. It might have one day made you the world's first trillionaire. Instead, you're wasting away here, in solitary confinement, wearing chains and a paper gown…and neither of us really understands why. Don't you at least want to try to know the answer?"

Baird did not reply.

"I'm hopeful that you can still achieve a degree of recovery, if only you will begin the journey by opening up to me. There's a genuine reason for optimism, Jonah." Dr. Cooper said. "The record shows that if not for your fast action on your brother's behalf, he would surely have been court-martialed and possibly sentenced to a lengthy stay in Fort Leavenworth. Instead, thanks to your connections in the White House, he got the psychiatric treatment he needed to recover fully. And he now enjoys a quiet, comfortable retirement with his wife in Virginia."

Baird remained silent.

"The last several years were probably unbearable for you, Jonah," Dr. Cooper said softly. "I get that. Now I'm trying to help you experience a recovery of your own. Your family history reveals a pattern of significant mental/emotional health issues, which, unfortunately, have surfaced in your life with tragic consequences. But I believe that, together, we can overcome them and you can experience peace and perhaps even fulfillment in the years you have left. So I appeal to you to please try to achieve it for yourself in whatever time you have left."

Baird finally, slowly raised his head, locked eyes with Dr. Cooper, and softly said, "I won't be here that long."

"On the contrary," Dr. Cooper replied. "You could be here the rest of your life."

"You don't get it, Doc," Baird softly said again and stared at the bay window in the doctor's office. "I'm telling you I won't be here long enough, and I'll bet you a million dollars I'm right."

The doctor guessed Baird was offering him a million dollars to help him escape via the window. Dr. Cooper believed it to be a legitimate offer, given what he knew about Baird having supposedly hidden most of his multi-billion-dollar fortune before he was apprehended.

"I must advise you not to repeat that," Dr. Cooper said

flatly. "If you do, I will have to report it as an attempt to bribe me, which will only make your time here even more unpleasant. My hope is that you will soon realize I'm offering you a far more valuable escape, Jonah," the doctor said in a final effort to reach Baird before he was returned to his cell. "And all it will cost you is to open yourself to defeating the demons that brought you here. I hope you will begin that journey next week."

Dr. Cooper then strode to the door and opened it for the guards who returned Baird to his dark, silent, windowless, five-by-eight cell for another week.

Moments later, the soft, shuffling sound of Baird's flip-flops in the hallway outside Dr. Cooper's office was replaced by the loud, pounding of the hard leather heels and soles of the boots worn by three perfectly pressed, spit-and-polish French Military Forces commandos who stood watch 24/7 over Legionnaire 1e Classe Gabriel Chastain, the delusional AWOL soldier who insisted he was "the one and only Nostradamus."

The commandos delivered their prisoner to Dr. Cooper's office in a rolling cylindrical, stainless steel cage barely big enough to contain the chiseled, battle-scarred, six-foot-four-inch, 240-pound hulk of a man. The French government ultimately agreed to the brief "Intake Interview" after hours of tense negotiations between the U.S. and French embassies.

The French government maintained it had sole authority over the Legionnaire during the short time he was to be held at the remote U.S. military detention center on the southern-most coast of Cuba. The Prescott administration, for its part, insisted that while the French prisoner was on U.S. soil, he must be physically and psychologically evaluated to ensure he was of sound body and mind until he was returned to France for a military trial. That was the singular concession agreed to by France's Ministry of Defense and President DuPris. So Dr. Cooper knew the session might be his only opportunity to probe the psyche of a soldier who was suffering from post-traumatic stress disorder so severe he believed he was the notorious French poet/prophet who died nearly 400 years earlier.

"Must he remain in that cage?" the doctor asked.

"Those are our orders," a guard said.

"Can I at least have some time alone with him?" the doctor asked, hopefully.

"I'm sorry, Doctor, but he must have French eyes on him at all times," one guard replied.

"But surely he's not going anywhere while caged like this," the doctor tried reasoning.

"He's escaped the cage three times already since he arrived," the guard said sheepishly. "But we don't know how."

"You know *nothing* about me," the prisoner boldly said in French. "You're all but steps to my ultimate objective. You will not deter me. You are powerless while I am among you!"

"Do you speak English?" the doctor asked in French.

"I speak many languages. But I'll not speak with you in any of them," the prisoner said.

"If you'll speak with me, I believe I can arrange for you to have some time free of that cage," the doctor offered.

"I can be free anytime I choose," the prisoner boasted.

"So why do you choose to be locked up like a wild animal?" the doctor probed skeptically.

"For your safety," the prisoner said, leering menacingly within the steel web.

Dr. Cooper wisely chose not to challenge that statement.

"I appreciate your candor and compassion, Nostradamus," he told the prisoner.

"I have no compassion. I have killed many men," the prisoner said. "But it is not yet time for the killing of Americans to begin."

"Do you know when that time will be?" the doctor felt compelled to ask.

"Soon," the prisoner said ominously. "Very soon."

"I would appreciate some warning, if you can provide it," the doctor tried to lighten the mood of the discussion.

"You'll not see me coming, Doctor," the prisoner said flatly. "That is my warning to you."

"How can you be so sure of all this?" the doctor probed a bit deeper.

"Would you like a demonstration of my power?" the prisoner asked, ominously.

"I-I suppose I would," the doctor asked with some hesitation and a glance at the guards, who had already gripped and released the safeties of their semi-automatic 9mm M1950 pistols.

"Relax gentlemen," the doctor said softly. "Remember…this is just a demonstration."

The guards did not relax, even as Dr. Cooper casually sat on the near corner of his desk.

"Okay, Nostradamus. You can escape anytime you're ready," he said confidently.

The prisoner stood stone-still at attention without touching the gate of his cage as it smoothly and quietly swung open with no apparent cause. Dr. Cooper stood up in wide-eyed amazement, and the guards drew their sidearms, crouched and took aim at the prisoner, who never moved a muscle until after the cage door closed and locked as mysteriously as it had opened.

"Would you like to see that again, Doctor?" the prisoner asked with a smirk.

"No, I've seen as much as I care to without some explanation from you regarding how you did that," Dr. Cooper replied.

"I am Nostradamus," the prisoner said boldly. "What further explanation do you need?"

"If you *are* Nostradamus, how is it that you're alive in the 21st century?" the doctor asked.

"I *am* Nostradamus. And the more important question is: How is anyone else in this room still alive?" the prisoner said in his deep, commanding voice.

"The French government says you are Legionnaire le Classe Gabriel Chastain," Dr. Cooper said. "They say you are a decorated military hero who sustained a serious brain injury in action and that you also suffer from post traumatic stress disorder. Is all of that not true?"

"You are all deceived," Nostradamus replied. "The Legionnaire died in action. He was a much different man than I. I would not have died as he did. I cannot be defeated."

"Now that I know what happened to Legionnaire Chastain, I have more questions than I ever imagined," Dr. Cooper said sincerely as he reached for a pen and writing tablet.

"I've tired of this conversation," the prisoner announced. "I wish to return to my lair."

"You mean *your cell*," one of the guards corrected him.

"Like this cage, a cell cannot contain me. I promise you," the prisoner snapped back.

"Can I look forward to another session with you next week?" Dr. Cooper asked.

"I won't be here that long," the prisoner said.

The hair on the back of the doctor's neck stood up when he heard the precise response that Baird had given earlier. The French guards returned their prisoner to his cell, unable to comprehend what they had just seen and heard in Dr. Cooper's office. But they were certain that whatever the truth was, Legionnaire 1e Classe Gabriel Chastain could not possibly do what they had just witnessed. So from then on, they called him Nostradamus, and they stood guard outside his cell with the unnerving feeling that he might simply walk out of it whenever he wished.

## 3

---

## FOUR CONQUESTS

The longer Doc sat on his front porch, the edgier he got. Q could feel it happening and tried to make small talk to calm him.

"I know you've heard this before, Doc, but this is an amazing view of the lake," he said. "Marsha and I can hardly wait for our place to be finished. Then I can stop envying you."

Doc didn't reply, and Q could see from the corner of his eye that Doc was intently scanning the landscape to the west.

"You can see just about every inch of shoreline from up here," Q said. "Did you realize that when you had this place built?"

"I counted on it," Doc said flatly. "I wanted exactly the advantage we have right now in case we ever needed it. I originally wanted to build on Wild Horse Island down below over there to the south. But the state wouldn't sell it to me. But this is the next best spot. The view is amazing, and it's like sitting in the corner of a room with a clear view of every entrance. If the Guardians come, we'll see 'em long before they get here."

Q scanned the landscape to the east, toward Rollins, an honest-to-God, 21$^{st}$ century, one-horse town with less than 200 folks in it. It wasn't yet 8:00 a.m., and US-93 was empty. But then suddenly…it wasn't.

"Helllllooooo?" Q said tentatively as he squinted at a far-off column of black vehicles approaching from the east. "You got your binoculars handy, Doc?" he asked calmly.

Doc raised his binoculars for a close look at the convoy.

"I'm willing to bet no one within 500 miles of here has ever seen a Conquest Knight XV," the former Navy SEAL said softly, "and here comes four of 'em."

"What the hell's a Conquest Knight XV?" Q predictably asked.

"It's a Canadian-build, 13,000-pound, fully armored SUV, and you're about to witness the havoc these MAHEMs can cause, my friend," Doc said ominously. "Flip the safety off and aim it just like a hunting rifle. But brace yourself against the wall before firing it because it kicks like a mule. Call Noah and Madeleine and tell them to get down here pronto. I'll wake Connie, and she'll take Marsha into the safe room with her. I'll get Louis and Jenny out here too."

"You got enough firepower for everybody?" Q asked as he speed-dialed Louis.

"There's plenty," Doc assured him and dashed into the house.

Noah and Madeleine were lodging in a fifth-wheel camper about a quarter-mile west of the lake house, while their home was being built. Q and Marsha had taken over the east wing of the lake house because they had yet to agree on a site for their new home over-looking the lake. And like true Marines, Louis and Jenny were holed-up in four large rooms in the rear of the house, ready and waiting for whatever came next.

"Wake up, Beauty," Doc said softly but firmly. "We've got unwelcome company. I'll explain later, I promise. But right now, you've got to wake up Marsha and get to the safe room."

"Why? What's wrong?" Connie mumbled as she strug-gled to awaken.

"I'll fill you in later, Beauty. I promise," Doc said anxiously. "But right now, just throw on a robe and get Marsha and yourself down below."

When Doc got back on the front porch, the SUVs were approaching single file about 100 yards away. He stood with his back flat against the house at one end of the porch while Q knelt at the other end with his back foot against the house. They trained their MAHEMs on the lead armored vehicle, which blocked their view of the others.

"Hold steady," Doc said calmly. "I'll put mine in his windshield at about 50 yards. If that doesn't shut him down, you do the same before he gets too close."

"Aye aye!" Q said simply and braced himself for the shock and awe to come.

Just then, Louis stepped onto the front porch with Jenny close behind.

"Mornin' folks," Doc said with his eyes locked on the lead SUV. "Hope you're ready for some fireworks."

"What kinda' vehicle is that?" Louis asked.

"The worst kind," Doc answered as he took aim, squeezed the MAHEM's trigger, and its molten metal payload rocketed toward the vehicle's windshield.

The men in the front seats of the SUV barely saw their deaths coming. The MAHEM shell caved-in the wind-shield, exploded into a bright flash, and a rolling cloud of dark black smoke with a force that blew out the side windows. The vehicle lurched left, careened wildly down the hill until it rolled four times in the direction of the lake.

"Looks like the Conquest company skimped on their glass," Q said sarcastically as he fired his MAHEM into the windshield of the second SUV with the same result as Doc's.

Meanwhile, Louis pulled another MAHEM out of the chest and loaded it. Then he released the safety, backed up against the house, and waited as Doc took aim at the third vehicle when it turned sharply in an evasive maneuver. That shell missed the side window, exploded just behind it, but did no visible damage to the vehicle's heavy armor.

"Damn!" Doc grunted in frustration.

"I got it," Louis calmly said, and fired the huge, cylindrical projectile that crashed through the center of the side window and exploded like those that penetrated the first two SUVs.

But the fourth Conquest plowed into the front porch. Doc, Q, Louis, and Jenny dove onto the grass and rolled in erratic directions to evade the shots the Guardians fired at them. Doc's weapons chest was catapulted off the porch onto the lawn, too, and he quickly opened the lid and took cover behind it. Q rolled under what was left of the porch, and Louis rolled under the SUV. Jenny —just under five and a half feet tall—scrambled to the rear of the vehicle, stood with her back pressed against it, and spotted an open gun port about six inches above her head.

"BOMB!?!" Jenny urgently signed to Louis, whose eyes were riveted on her.

"What bomb?" he signed back to her from the ground just as urgently.

"BOMB IN CHEST?" she signed back to him.

Louis quickly slid from under the SUV and bolted to the chest, sliding tight against Doc.

"You got grenades in this box?" Louis asked Doc.

"Some," Doc answered.

"V40 minis?" Louis shot back.

"A few," Doc answered and scooped three V40s out of the chest while shots rang out and bullets ricocheted off its lid.

Louis took them from Doc and hurriedly rolled the tiny, round grenades to Jenny, who had taken his place under the SUV. She stuffed the tiny grenades into her shirt and scrambled back to the rear of the vehicle. As she had guessed, the grenades' 1.6-inch diameter was small enough to fit through the gun port.

"One...two!" she counted after pulling the pins and dropped them into the SUV and jammed fingers into her ears.

Even encased in the Conquest's heavy armor plating, the blast from the V40s was deafening. The immense concussion they generated blew-out the windows of the cab and ejected one Guardian out onto the SUV's hood. He was badly wounded and nearly dead when Q lifted the man's left arm and pulled up a still-smoking jacket sleeve to reveal the all-too-familiar "GUARDIAN" tattoo on the inside of the man's wrist.

"Well, they're back," Doc sighed. "That means the Keeper will be back soon too."

"How do you know that?" Louis asked.

"Because this is the Keeper's war, not theirs," Doc reasoned. "They don't get paid, and they have no skin in the game as long as he's locked up and they don't have to answer to him. So if he's not on the loose already, you can bet he soon will be."

"Homeland Security's got a mess to clean up in your front yard this morning," Q said with a chuckle. "The president owes you for a whole lot of sod. And Connie's going to be pissed when she sees her porch."

"I can always count on you to see the bright side," Doc grumbled.

"Sorry, Doc," Q sighed. "I'll work on that."

"The president's going to want to advise Gitmo command asap," Louis said. "And Doc, you should consider trying to restore one of these Conquests. New ones go for around $800,000, and it just might come in handy sometime."

"Really? $800,000?" Doc replied with eyes wide. "It might be a project *you* take on if you believe you'd have a use for it. But I'm out of this business the minute we put the Keeper away once and for all.

"Q, call the Sheriff's Office and Homeland Security and get them out here," Doc said. "I'll call the president and tell him we have a brand-new battle on our hands. I'll arrange to have his personal plane waiting for us at Malmstrom Air Force Base in the morning to take us to D.C. Tonight we all pack and batten down the hatches here, because we'll be gone until this war is finished. This time, we're taking the battle to Baird and his Guardians. When this war is over, days like this are over for Connie and me."

Connie threw open the safe room door as Doc approached, and she gave him a bear hug.

"Thank God, you're all okay!" she yelled. "We watched it all on closed-circuit TV. It was horrifying! Doc, what are we going to do? Will we ever be safe!"

"Everything's going to be just fine, I promise you, Beauty," Doc told his wife sincerely. "I promise you we're going to bring this chaos to an end."

Doc pulled Marsha into his hug with Connie and told her, "Q and I intend to handle this the way we should have handled it from the start. Up until now, we've let the president, the military, and the Justice Department handle things their way. And we haven't slept peacefully since this insanity began. That ends now!"

Back outside, Connie and Marsha joined the others who were awaiting the arrival of the sheriff's deputies and agents of Homeland Security. Doc slipped into the backyard and called the President.

"Hello, Mr. President," Doc said urgently. "Have you heard anything from Gitmo this morning?"

"No, why, Doc?" the president asked. "Is everything okay there?"

"It is right now," Doc said flatly. "We just repelled quite a contingent of Guardians at the lake house and came out of it unharmed."

"Guardians?!" President Prescott shot back over the phone. "More Guardians have surfaced? How many?"

"We're still counting the bodies, Mr. President," Doc said. "And I think we'll have a lot more of them very soon. I also believe you'll hear from Gitmo shortly because this can only mean the Keeper is about to break out...or he has already."

"Doc. Be rational." the president replied. "No one's ever escaped from Gitmo. It's impossible."

"Mr. President, it might *seem* impossible," Doc said, "but it seems equally impossible that the Guardians would know Baird's status. And I'm telling you they would not have shown up at the lake house today unless they knew Baird is about to return. Trust me on this.

"I've activated my team," Doc told the president. "We're packing and closing up the house this afternoon. Will you be in Washington tomorrow?"

"I will be, yes," the president replied. "Can you be here by early afternoon if I send my personal plane? I can have it at Glacier Park International Airport, ready for takeoff by 0700. I will brief you when you get here."

"Perfect!" Doc replied. "I'll see you by midday and have the team at Gitmo before nightfall. If it's available, I would appreciate your lending Connie and Marsh use of Camp David until we hunt Baird down."

"It's theirs for as long as they need it, Doc. Have you alerted Homeland Security?" President Prescott asked.

"I have, and thank you, Mr. President," Doc answered. "Mr. President, I give you my word that we will see justice done."

"I'm confident you will, Doc," the president replied. "I'll see you soon!"

"Thank you, Mr. President," Doc replied as the president ended the call.

Doc tucked his phone away and rejoined the team in the front yard.

"We've been activated, folks!" he announced. "We'll fly to D.C. out of Glacier International at 0700 tomorrow."

"You don't plan to leave Marsha and me here, do you?" Connie asked quickly.

"I've saved the best for last," Doc told her. "You and Marsha will have Camp David all to yourselves until we finish this."

"We need to talk, Doc," Q said quietly.

"What's up?" Doc asked.

"The Guardian who ended up on the hood of the SUV mumbled something that could be important."

"What'd he say?" Doc asked anxiously.

"He said, 'You cannot save your president,'" Q replied.

"What? What does that mean? Did he say anything else?" Doc excitedly asked.

"He said, 'It is written in the scrolls,'" Q answered.

"In the scrolls? What scrolls?" Doc asked even more anxiously. "What does that mean?"

"That's what I asked him," Q shot back, "and he said, 'Nostradamus has written in the scrolls that the president will die.'"

"So the president was right again," Doc said. "The Nostradamus character *is* mixed up with Baird and his Guardians," Doc said, running a hand through his hair in exasperation. "The president never should have agreed to lock up that madman at Gitmo while Baird is there."

# 4

# A MATCH MADE IN HELL

The four cells in the solitary confinement wing of the U.S. Guantanamo Military Detention Center on the southeastern tip of Cuba each had a ceiling-mounted closed-circuit camera. Every shift, one of the guards assigned to the section continually walked up and down the corridor outside the cells and viewed detainees through the slot in the door every three minutes. Baird was in Cell 2. The French Legionnaire, who insisted he was Nostradamus, was in Cell 3. In addition to the American guards, French Republican Guardsmen Raphael Caron, Jules Brodeur, and Alexandre Moreau alternated eight-hour shifts just outside Nostradamus's cell at all times to ensure he did not attempt to harm himself or escape. There seemed to be no chance of Baird or Nostradamus surprising and overpowering their guards. Still, they managed to do just that.

At 1203 hours, a guard looked into Baird's cell and saw him writhing on the floor.

"Going in!" the guard shouted to the two others seated at opposite ends of the hall.

He quickly unlocked Baird's cell door, and the other two guards followed him in. Meanwhile, while Guardsman Caron was distracted by the commotion, the door of Nostradamus's cell silently slid open. The towering supposed-prophet exited his cell without making a sound and wrapped his arms in a chokehold around Caron's throat.

"One false move and I'll snap your neck!" Nostradamus whispered forcefully. "Now, walk!" Nostradamus said and forced Caron forward toward Cell 2.

The two of them filled Cell 2's doorway, behind the two American guards who were focused on the lead guard as he knelt over Baird and shined a penlight into his eyes.

"He's having a seizure!" he shouted. "Radio the command center for the doctor!"

"Do not do that," Nostradamus said forcefully in perfect English.

His words and sudden presence stunned the guards, and they momentarily froze.

"You're far too easy!" Baird sneered at the guards as he jumped to his feet. "We make a great team, don't we, Nostradamus?" he asked excitedly.

"You won't get away with this!" a guard shouted. "There's no escaping Gitmo!"

"Not without your help," Nostradamus told him and tightened his chokehold around his captive's throat. "Now gather 'round and walk with us out to the courtyard."

Baird ripped the radios off all the guards, except Caron. Then he took their pistols and handcuffs. He tossed the weapons onto his bed and cuffed his three guards together around him. Then he maneuvered his human shields close beside his new partner in crime and said, "Okay, fellas. Let's take a walk."

Being cuffed together in a circle around Baird made it difficult for the guards to walk. But Baird knew it also made it impossible for the marksmen waiting for him in the yard to shoot him without the risk of also shooting a guard. In the Central Command Office, Detention Center Commander Lieutenant Colonel Reginald Williams watched the prisoners' every move via the closed-circuit cameras and hurriedly worked his way through the escape protocol in a desperate effort to get a step ahead of the prisoners before they reached the yard.

"Get Secretary McDonnaly on the phone, now!" Commander Williams ordered young Corporal Garrison Hooper, standing at the ready nearby.

"Yes, sir!" Corporal Hooper answered and leaped to the phone.

"Stand down!" Commander Williams ordered guards within the Highest Security Unit over the radio. "Do not engage the prisoners. I repeat: Stand down! Attention Perimeter Command: Assume security positions and await my orders! Lieutenant Waters, get Guardsmen Moreau and Brodeur up here on the double!"

"Yes, sir!" the lieutenant answered and sprinted out of the Command Center.

Baird and Nostradamus weren't surprised by the empty hallways leading to the exercise compound. They knew the Command Center staff was watching their every move. When the deadly partners and their hostages stepped into the bright sunlight in the yard, they could clearly see the half-dozen rifles trained on them in the guard towers. Nostradamus squeezed his captive's neck even tighter. He walked with erratic strides, jerked his captive from side-to-side, and a couple of times spun completely around. Baird crouched among the three handcuffed guards, and they copied the Frenchman's moves.

"Do not approach the front gate!" Commander Williams shouted over the loudspeaker as he intently watched the desperate men move across the yard and make their way closer and closer to freedom in the bright, hot sunlight of that Cuban afternoon.

Nostradamus led the way with Guardsman Caron gasping for air in a chokehold that was tighter than ever. When the mad man and Baird reached the main gate with their hostages in tow, Commander Williams spoke softly over the radio to the six marksmen.

"Lock onto X if you can," he said softly. "But hold your fire, and do not target the Frenchmen. We must avoid an international incident at all costs. Is that understood?"

"Understood in Tower One," the marksman in the tower responded, and each of the others did so in turn.

"Bring us a jeep and open this gate, or this worm I hold will die!" Nostradamus said firmly into the open mic of his captive's radio.

The massive Frenchman lifted Caron off the ground by the neck and mashed the helpless Guardsman's chest and face into the course, hot chain link of the main gate.

"Damn it!" Commander Williams grunted under his breath as he watched helplessly.

He knew he was powerless at that moment. He was not about to risk the lives of the four guards who were at the mercy of his two most-desperate and dangerous prisoners.

"Commander! I have President Prescott and Secretary McDonnaly on the phone, sir!" Corporal Hooper said as he handed Commander Williams the phone.

The call came through at precisely the last possible moment as Commander Williams had to quickly decide whether or not to risk releasing Baird and Nostradamus into the Cuban countryside, whether to give them an "escape jeep" and open the gate...or open fire.

"Commander Williams, this is President Prescott," the Commander-in-Chief said firmly. "Do not engage these two! We have options beyond your resources. So let them go wherever it is they think they're going and we'll round them up again soon enough. Is that clear?"

"Perfectly, Mr. President," Commander Williams said firmly and hit the "Open" button that released the detention center's main gate. "Hold your fire!" he stated firmly one more time to the marksmen in the towers.

Seeing the gate open, the motor pool quickly pulled the "escape jeep" up to it. The commander was relieved to see Nostradamus and Baird release the hostages before driving away. The pair would soon learn the jeep they were in was rigged to go no faster than 25 miles per hour and had only a half-gallon of gas in the tank.

"Thank you for your fast response, Mr. President. I assume you saw them leave. We stand ready for your orders. They won't get far in that jeep, and we'll have a surveillance drone in the air to track them in minutes."

"No need, Commander," the President replied. "We already have an ultra-high-altitude fix on them, and we're in the White House Situation Room watching them as we speak. So a drone's not necessary. Officially, we don't even have drones on the island, and I don't want a call from the Cuban Embassy asking me when that changed."

"Understood, Sir!" Commander Williams replied with a sigh of relief.

"Were any French Republican Guardsmen injured?" the president asked.

"One slightly, sir," Commander Williams replied. "Chastain overpowered Guardsmen Raphael Caron and held him in a vicious chokehold since this whole thing started."

"But no U.S. personnel have engaged with Chastain?" the president asked hopefully.

"That is correct, Mr. President," Commander Williams replied. "We have only engaged Prisoner X. But as you can see, we've had no success."

"On the contrary, Commander," the president said cheerfully, "you've had very important success! The protocols you have in place, which your team followed perfectly, slowed these two vicious criminals enough for us to get ahead of them…and you safeguarded our promise to the French government. So to you and the people under your command, I say, WELL DONE!"

"Thank you, Mr. President!" Commander Williams said as he snapped to attention. "I will be sure to forward your message to everyone here, sir."

"Are French Republican Guardsmen Brodeur and Moreau with you?" the president asked.

"They are now, Mr. President," Commander Williams

said as he watched them stride quickly into the Command Center. "Would you like to speak with them, Mr. President?"

"Put me on speakerphone, Commander," the president said.

"TEN-HUT!" Commander Williams pronounced firmly and brought the American forces in the Command Center to attention, then put the phone on "Speaker."

"This is President of the United States Donald Prescott," the president began. "Guardsmen Brodeur and Moreau, I pledge the full force of the American government in support of your recapturing Legionnaire 1e Classe Gabriel Chastain as quickly as possible. I have already assured President DuPris that Commander Williams and those under his command stand ready to assist you in any way necessary, consistent with our original understanding that Legionnaire Chastain is to be afforded all the rights and protections of a citizen, a soldier—and a hero—of France. Do either of you have any questions or requests for me at this time?"

"No, Mr. President," the guardsmen both replied.

"Then I join President DuPris in wishing you both Godspeed in accomplishing this important mission, gentlemen. Be safe!" the president said as Brodeur and Moreau headed out of the Command Center to begin their pursuit of Nostradamus.

"Commander Williams, I must speak with you privately for a moment," the president said.

"I'm here, Mr. President," the commander said and turned off the speaker function.

"Commander, I can't stress strongly enough how urgent it is that these two escapees be captured," the president said calmly. "Each of them poses a grave danger to the public and can do great damage to international relations among several nations. Working together, the danger they pose to society is impossible to overstate."

"I understand, Mr. President," the commander replied. "We'll bring them to justice."

"That won't be easy," the president said. "But I know you'll do your best to work with the guardsman without bringing the wrath of France down on us. To make matters worse, our escapees appear to be headed into rough terrain and bad weather. So we'll lose sight of them shortly. Defense Secretary Jameson and Secretary McDonnaly are in the Situation Room and will stay on this secure line with you as long as we can maintain the satellite uplink. When we lose that, I'm afraid you'll be on your own until we can re-establish contact. I'm turning you over to Secretaries Jameson and McDonnaly now. Godspeed and go get'em, Commander."

"Thank you again, Mr. President," the commander said and activated the pursuit party with a clear, decisive hand signal to Captain James Sorrels, his second-in-command.

The captain raced to the motor pool leading a 12-member team to six fueled and idling ATVs. As the team raced out the front gate, the captain could see the two guardsmen ahead at full gallop atop the jet black Merens ponies they'd brought to Gitmo with them. The horses had caused a lot of talk and eye-rolling among the American troops at the time. Now, Captain Sorrels realized the muscular mounts were perfect for tracking the fugitives in the mountains.

"We just lost our uplink," Defense Secretary Jameson told Captain Sorrels over the secure line patched to his radio, "but we saw them run out of gas about a mile ahead of you, in the direction of the mountains to the northeast."

Through his binoculars, Sorrels saw the guardsman ride-up on the abandoned jeep, then cut their ponies sharply to the east.

"Follow them!" Sorrels shouted at his driver. "Just like we figured, X and the French Creep are headed for the mountains!"

But that was only partly correct because the convicts had no interest in the mountains. The Guantanamo land leased from Cuba is bordered by well-grated, hard-packed gravel roads that stretch out for miles and are perfectly straight wherever possible. The last half-mile on the southeast corner is the straightest of all and stretches to within 50 feet of the ocean.

Baird and Nostradamus had nearly reached that stretch

of road when their jeep ran out of gas. That was the first moment that Baird experienced any doubt concerning the mental powers of his new partner.

"Why didn't he see this coming?" Baird silently asked himself. "What else is he missing?" was understandably his next question.

But there was no doubting that Nostradamus had made their escape possible. So Baird shoved his questions aside and was all-in on whatever his partner's next moves might be. After all, it was a fact that Baird had arranged to have a plane waiting for them near the end of that road based upon Nostradamus's supernatural assurance that the two of them would be free and racing to meet it at that very time. And here there were, on foot, but within running distance to the Guardian pilot waiting for them in a small, sleek, fast, 2000 Seawind 350 land and seaplane with its engine running and ready for take-off.

Brodeur and Moreau could barely hold of the reins as their Merens raced to catch up with Baird and Nostradamus, who had abandoned the jeep and were running toward the Seawind. Brodeur and Moreau both emptied their 20-shell clips at the Seawind as it taxied and lifted into the air. But they were standing in the stir-rups of ponies racing full-out, and too far away to hit the plane. By the time Captain Williams and his men caught up with the two Frenchmen, they heard the Seawind's 350 horsepower engine in the distance, but none of them could make it out as it gained speed and altitude in the bright, sun-washed, midday sky.

"Well, there goes our perfect record of no escapes," Williams sighed and grabbed his radio.

"I'm sorry, Mr. Secretary, but they had a light plane waiting for them, and we've lost 'em," Williams told Secretary of State McDonnaly.

"It's okay, Captain," the secretary assured him. "We figured they'd leave the island as quickly as possible. We've got two E3 Sentry surveillance radar aircraft in the air, each circling in a 50-mile radius off the north and the south ends of the island. If they're in the air anywhere between Puerto Rico and the Florida Keys, we'll have 'em in our sites shortly."

"Hunt them down, Mr. Secretary," the captain said. "That's a partnership made in hell."

"Don't worry, Captain. They won't get far," the secretary said confidently. "We do this sort of thing better than anybody. I'll update the president. In the meantime, make sure the French Republican Guardsmen are okay...and have fun with the paperwork."

## 5

# A TEXAS SHOOTOUT

T he Guardian, who piloted the Seawind, was very aware that he had one of the best jobs in Baird's Guardian army. All it required was a pilot's license and total obedience, which, like just about everything he enjoyed, was paid for by Baird. Money gave Baird his power, power to free himself and Chastain from Gitmo, power for the pair to live out their psychotic delusions as the Keeper and Nostradamus, power to create the evil they unleashed and escape the justice they deserved. Whether calling himself "the Keeper" was a delusion or a mere masquerade, his stealth and deception were very real. The crimes his power unleashed were grotesque and intentional. His murders were especially so.

Chastain's power was even more fearsome because money could not buy it...or stop it. His power was not fabricated, manipulated, or orchestrated. It rose from the ashes of a traumatic psychological coup d 'etat that imprisoned his heart and mind. Chastain never met Nostradamus. Nostradamus never dreamed of Chastain. The shattered Legionnaire paratrooper was a victim of a Nostradamus delusion, haunted by dreams of the world's future, while oblivious to his own recent past. His evildoings were never planned, and his victims were merely collateral damage.

So the bond between this vicious duo was forged in the collision of two powerful forces of evil: One obsessed with schemes to mold the world however he wished, the other haunted by dreams of the world as he believed it was destined to be. And now they were racing to begin their reign of terror. Baird's almost limitless money was delivering everything they needed to put their plans in motion. And Chastain's imprisoned mind was sadly unaware of all that his enslaved body was going to do to help this evil partnership survive and prosper.

Baird told the pilot to rendezvous with a fuel tanker truck that was waiting for them at Marco Island Executive Airport, just south of Florida's Old Marco Junction, then hightail it to Tampa Bay, where an AirFish 8 seaplane was waiting for Baird and Chastain to climb aboard.

Chastain dozed off halfway to Tampa Bay, and, as he had while sleeping at Gitmo, he saw an AirFish seaplane waiting to fly Baird and him across the Gulf of Mexico to Somerville Lake, northwest of Houston, Texas. In Chastain's dream, the gleaming white, manta ray-shaped plane flew at nearly 400 miles per hour, just five feet above the surface of the water, a maneuver designed to frustrate the military's ability to track the plane's movements. In his dream, Chastain saw the craft rendezvous with a second SeaFish on Sommerville Lake to refuel. But Chastain awoke, and the vision ended when the plane landed on Tampa Bay. So he didn't foresee what would happen after the plane crossed the gulf and landed on the Texas lake three hours later.

The futuristic ten-seater approached Somerville Lake fast and low, from the south just above the trees. It's broad, angular delta wings gave it the look of a gliding bird of prey. The air ship's tail was a trailing wing perched atop two 15-foot struts, which gave it its super maneuverability, even at slower speeds as it hugged the ground or glided just above the waves.

Texas Game Wardens Justin Markham and Carlos Riaz didn't hear the plane's muffled engine during a routine patrol in a skiff along the southern shore until the AirFish flew directly over them, and barely cleared a stand of Mexican White Oak trees at nearly 150 miles per hour.

"What the hell is that?" Markham gasped, having never seen an AirFish before.

The plane came in so fast and low; the wardens thought it was a crash landing. Markham was at the controls, so he gripped the wheel, yelled, "Hang on!" and jammed the throttle completely open. The jolt almost threw Riaz from his seat as the skiff's bow rose up, and it rocketed in the direction of the plane.

"We've got company, Keeper," the Guardians pilot said over his shoulder.

"No need to panic," Baird replied. "We've handled threats a lot tougher than this haven't we? Stay calm."

"What will you do?" Chastain asked. "Will you kill them, or just sink their boat?"

"You're the one who can see the future," Baird said with a sly smile. "You tell me!"

Markham and Rias were a little more than 500 yards away when the AirFish came to a graceful stop on the water and a second plane exactly like it approached from the north.

"We've never seen one before, and now there's two of them," Rias told Markham.

"They look like mighty expensive planes," Markham thought out loud. "So the question is: Are they just out having a good time on the water, or are they up to something?"

"My gut tells me it's the latter," Riaz replied.

"That makes it unanimous," Markham said and slowed the skiff so as not to alarm the people aboard the planes.

Both wardens unsnapped the straps on their 40-caliber, semi-automatic Glocks, but left them holstered. Riaz quickly lifted their Daniel Defense M4 rifles out of the cargo bin beside him and laid them on the deck nearby, but out of view.

"Don't get nervous," Baird said over the radio to both Guardian pilots. "We're just here to refuel and be on our way. Don't do anything rash."

"Keeper, refueling is illegal on the water like this," the second Guardian pilot said softly. "So, what do we tell them we're out here for?"

"Nostradamus and I will stay out of sight, and you're just a couple of AirFish owners admiring each other's planes," Baird said. "It doesn't have to be more complicated than that."

Riaz rose out of his seat and stood beside Markham to get a better look at the planes.

"What are you thinking, partner?" Riaz asked.

"I'm thinking this could be just about anything…or nothing at all," Markham replied with squinted eyes. "Cool but careful," he said softly. "Be cool but careful."

"I'm with you," Riaz said just as softly.

As the skiff closed to 50 yards out, Riaz and Markham were on full alert.

"Texas Parks and Wildlife Wardens Riaz and Markham just stopping by to say, 'Welcome!'" Markham announced over the bullhorn as the skiff slowed and came to a stop between the two planes.

The Guardian pilot of the second plane to arrive stuck his head and an arm out the cockpit window and casually waved to the wardens.

"Howdy!" the Guardian shouted to them.

"What brings you to Sommerville Lake reservoir?" Markham asked. "Fishing or just some fun in the sun? Or are you having mechanical issues?"

"Just enjoying a new lake and meeting a fellow AirFish owner," the Guardian answered.

"Is that what these sweet things are called?' Riaz asked. "They almost look like they belong in outer space."

"Yeah, they're brand new," the Guardian said. "We're lucky to have two of the first prototypes. They're pretty amazing."

"You can say that again," Markham responded. "Could I see your pilot's license and some form of photo ID, please?"

"Easy. Relax. Just do what he asks," Baird said softly over the radio.

"Sure," the Guardian said and took both out of his logbook on the seat beside him.

When Markham brought the skiff alongside the cockpit and reached up for the documents, the Guardian spotted the semi-automatic rifles on the deck and became very nervous. Meanwhile, Markham noted the

"Guardian" tattoo on the inside of the pilot's wrist. It seemed curious, but it meant nothing to him.

"They're armed to the teeth!" the Guardian anxiously whispered into the radio while Markham checked out his documents.

"Take it easy!" Baird quietly said again. "They most likely always have weapons with them. There's no reason to panic."

"Don't go anywhere," Markham said as he handed the documents back to the Guardian.

"Sure thing, officer," the Guardian replied as casually as he could manage.

Riaz pushed the boat off from the plane, and Markham expertly maneuvered it in the direction of the other AirFish.

"I don't have my pilot's license with me," the Guardian behind the controls of Baird's plane whispered.

"What?!" Baird whispered. "How could you screw up like this, you idiot?!"

"I'm sorry, Keeper," was all the Guardian managed to say.

"I would shoot you here and now if I could!" Baird shouted at him.

"Calm down!" Chastain said as loudly as he dared. "Maybe they won't ask for it."

"Of course, they'll ask for it!" Baird shot back. "We have to get off this plane right now! And I can't swim!"

"Are you serious?" Chastain replied as he silently opened the cockpit door. "You're coming with me whether you can swim or not. Hang on to me any way you can."

Chastain slipped silently into the chilly water and signaled Baird to join him. Reluctantly, Baird slipped into the water and wrapped an arm around Chastain's muscular neck.

"Hold your breath," Chastain whispered to his shivering partner. "I'm going to swim under the plane."

"Wha….?!" Baird was interrupted when they both disappeared underwater.

While Markham pulled the skiff alongside the second plane, Chastain and Baird quietly swam under the craft's broad wings.

"Can I see your pilot's license and a photo ID, please?" Markham asked the Guardian.

"Well, here's my driver's license," the Guardian said, "but I'm afraid I don't have my pilot's license with me."

Riaz quietly slipped behind Markham and slowly drew his pistol.

"Do you know this license is expired?" Markham quickly asked.

"No! No, I didn't realize that!" the Guardian said nervously. "I guess I'm really in violation, aren't I?"

"I'm afraid you are," Markham confirmed. "What did you plan to do today?"

"What do you mean?" the Guardian asked, even more nervously.

"Why are you here?" Markham asked calmly. "I see you have no passengers. Neither does the other pilot. Seems like a lot of plane to fly empty."

"Well…well, we just thought it would be great to meet here and compare planes," the Guardian said anxiously and began to fidget.

"Where are you based?" Markham asked.

"Lake Ray Hubbard, just outside of Dallas," the Guardian said honestly because Baird was no longer there to tell him what else to say.

"Nice area," Markham said casually. "Where's the other pilot based?"

"Ah…ah…now that you ask, I realize I don't know," the Guardian said. "We connected online about a week ago, and I don't remember him ever saying where he was based. B-but he suggested we meet here. So I figure he's within 400 miles of home."

"Makes sense," Markham replied with a shrug. "What's his name?"

"What?" the Guardian shot back.

"What's the other pilot's name?" Markham asked.

"I don't know his name," the Guardian answered. "He goes by 'Guardian' online."

Markham accepted that because of the other pilot's tattoo. But Riaz wrapped his hand around the grip of his Glock and readied himself to use it if the situation continued to go south.

"Well, you know, his ID says he's from Phoenix," Markham said without blinking.

"Phoenix? Wow!" the Guardian said. "He's come a long way."

"I'm afraid I can't allow you to fly out of here until we can verify that you're properly licensed," Markham told the Guardian. "So I have to ask you to follow me back to our office, onshore. I'm sure we can straighten this out in no time."

"Okay—I guess," the Guardian sighed and began to sweat profusely.

The Guardian started his engine and slowly pulled away from the other AirFish to give Markham room to take the lead in the skiff. At least, that's what he and Riaz thought.

"This smells awful fishy," Riaz commented. "No pun intended."

"I hear ya'," Markham answered. "I just hope we're both wrong."

But they weren't wrong.

"Get out of here right now!" Baird shouted to the Guardian over the radio. "If they get you ashore, they'll lock you up for sure."

As soon as the warden's had their backs to the plane, the Guardian throttled up, and the plane quickly accelerated.

"Shut it down!" Markham shouted into the bullhorn. "Shut it down now!"

As Riaz aimed his 44 at the plane, he found himself looking down both barrels of a sawed-off shotgun the Guardian had stuck out the cockpit window. Markham saw the weapon too and accelerated the skiff into an evasive maneuver. The move may have saved them both because the Guardian fired both barrels and tore a six-inch hole in the starboard side of the boat.

Riaz dropped to the floor of the skiff, grabbed one of the semi-automatic carbines, and emptied its 30-round clip into the plane's engine compartment in the hope of shutting it down before it lifted off the lake.

"We're taking on a lot of water!" he shouted to Markham and emptied the second carbine's clip into the seaplane as it began lifting into the air.

"We are not letting this guy leave," Markham shouted to Riaz.

"But we can't stay afloat much longer, Justin!" Riaz shouted back as he watched the lake water rush into the skiff from the gaping hole in its side.

"Grab the grappling hook!" Markham shouted and steered the skiff directly at the accelerating plane that was now about three feet above the lake and quickly rising.

Riaz snatched the 30-pound grappling hook from the stern of the skiff, leaped to his feet, and began twirling the nasty-looking hook over his head by the chain attached to it.

"Throw it at the tail!" Markham yelled as the skiff closed within 15 feet of the AirFish, which was now at least ten feet in the air. "Throw it, Carlos! Give it your best shot and bail out!"

Carlos launched the grappling hook, and it clanged loudly as it wrapped around the closer of the plane's two tail struts and took hold. As it did, Riaz dove into the lake, with Markham right behind him.

With the sinking skiff tethered to its tail, the plane tried mightily to remain airborne. But it smashed into the lake about 100 yards away and burst into flames. Suddenly, Markham heard the sound of the other seaplane's engine fading behind him, and he spun in the water.

"Damn!" he grunted and shook the lake water from his hair as he wrestled with the reality that he and Riaz had stumbled onto something evil going down…and it had slipped through their fingers.

"Don't take this too hard, Justin," Riaz said as he tread water nearby. "We lived through it! And as for the pilots: Stopping one out of two ain't bad."

"Since you're so upbeat about this, I'll leave it to you to do the paperwork," Markham said as he watched the burning AirFish sink into the lake. "There's no way that poor bastard lived through that," he said softly.

The wardens then watched the second plane fade into the clouds in the west before they began the swim to shore.

"You know, I served in the Navy with a captain who always said everything happens for a reason," Markham said as they swam. "I wasn't convinced then, and I'm still not convinced."

"And that's the reason I'm doing the paperwork," Riaz chuckled and kept swimming.

## 6

---

## THE HIDDEN SCROLLS

As Doc led his team aboard the president's personal 757 the sixth time, he found it oddly funny that the experience still felt as welcome, yet uncomfortable, as it did. The contrast may have been amplified by having to walk through the noisy, sparse surroundings of Glacier Park International Airport, then stepping aboard the $100 million-dollar Dreamliner of Donald James Prescott, one of the world's wealthiest businessmen, and now 46th President of the United States.

It was one thing to fly somewhere aboard an impersonal, run-of-the-mill airliner. It was quite another matter to be warmly welcomed by a genuinely friendly flight crew as his team stepped into the Dreamliner. Few things about being onboard felt like riding in an airplane. The experience felt more like relaxing in a combination penthouse and Ferrari with wings. That was the inevitable first impression of the luxuriously appointed cabin with its large, high-back glove-soft leather chairs and sofas bathed in warm, ambient lighting that danced off highly polished mahogany and 24-carat gold fixtures, which seemed to be everywhere.

Beyond the main cabin, there was an eight-seat theatre, a 12-seat conference room, a full bath, and two spacious bedrooms. The aircraft cruises at just under 600 miles per hour, thanks to its two powerful Rolls Royce jet engines. So Doc figured they'd be in D.C. by noon.

"Who's up for a light breakfast?" Mary, the youngest crewmember asked as cheerfully as ever, and laughed when everyone's arm, including hers, shot in the air.

She and Portia, the veteran of the crew, loved having Doc's team aboard. Unlike President Prescott, who was always all-business, Doc's bunch never talked about what they did. Instead, they brought aboard stories of meeting interesting characters while exploring picturesque Zurich, Switzerland, and historic Savannah, Georgia, of catching cod six feet long by the light of the moon in the Bering Strait. But most of all, Mary and Portia loved talking with Connie and Marsha about having found bargains while antique hunting in far-flung places.

As always, the team insisted that Portia and Mary enjoy breakfast with them around the conference table, and the conversation was fast and fun. Doc was grateful for that because he knew it, at least briefly, took Connie's mind off the events of the day before. It also gave him the chance to slip off unnoticed and spend a few solitary minutes thinking in the quiet of the theater. He still hadn't come to terms with his many mixed feelings about this being his last mission. He felt ready for a slower, safer life. Even more important, he knew Connie was too.

But serving his country was the only life Doc had ever known. And to him, serving didn't mean pushing a pencil and papers around a desk, not by a longshot. A piece of him had always known serving wouldn't last forever. And besides, his days as a soldier of fortune had made him and Connie—and the rest of the team— multi-millionaires. Louis and Jenny were exceptions. They were active Marines deployed to the team by the president himself. And their heroics on their one and only mission with the team so far had earned them both significant promotions. There was no doubt their military careers were headed in the right direction. So the math told Doc this visit to the White House was the ideal opportunity to inform the president he would retire once Baird was brought to justice once and for all.

So there he sat, resting his chin on his hand, staring into the silent, black 60-inch flat-screen on the wall in front of him, when Q slipped into the reclining seat beside him and handed him a pair of Bluetooth headphones.

"Portia is patching the president into the screen," he told Doc. "He's got an update for us."

"I'll bet you a popsicle Baird's escaped again," Doc said and slipped the headphones on.

"I'm partial to creamsicles, myself," Q said with his predictably bad humor and slipped his headphones on too.

The screen in front of them came to life with the Seal of the President of the United States.

"Standby for the president," a voice said calmly through their headphones

The small, red LED light beside the camera atop the screen told the pair they were visible on the White House end of the connection. Doc and Q both instinctively straightened in their seats and braced themselves for what the President was about to tell them.

"Hello, gentlemen!" the president bellowed in his usual cheerful tone. "I know you'll be here shortly, but we're suddenly struggling to gain control of a situation before it explodes into a full-blown international incident, and I want to update you before you touch down."

"I've already bet Q that you're about to tell us Baird has escaped again," Doc said with a warry smile. "Did I win, Mr. President?"

"I'm afraid you did, Doc," the president said. "But the news is far worse than that. I just conducted a debriefing with Gitmo Detention Center Commander Lieutenant Colonel Reginald and learned that Baird now poses more danger to our nation and the world than ever before."

"That can only mean the Legionnaire escaped with

him," Doc sighed. "Just as that loony Frenchmen said he would."

"Did they get off the island, Mr. President?" Q asked, fearing the answer.

"They did," the president replied. "We've tracked them with an E3 Sentry since they left the island in a small seaplane. They're headed north, in the direction of the Keys. But our bet is they'll keep going to the mainland and put down for fuel somewhere outside either Homestead, on the Atlantic coast, or Everglades City on the Gulf. We'll know which shortly. We've notified local police, the sheriffs' departments, and state police, and we've mobilized Homeland Security on both coasts."

"Are they armed?" Doc asked, knowing the answer.

"You know they must be," the president replied.

"Do you have any idea where their ultimate destination is?" Q asked.

"We figure Chastain's hell-bent on returning to Sedona, Arizona," the president replied.

"Why do you say that, exactly, Mr. President?" Doc asked.

"The FBI and France's DGSE yanked him out of there last week with just the clothes on his back," the president explained. "He complained about having left behind some sort of scrolls he claims prove he's Nostradamus, and that he's accurately predicted the who, what, when and where of the assassinations of French President DuPris—and me. So on top of being delusional, it appears he's also an egomaniac determined to show the world how amazing he is."

"He sounds like a fruitcake to me," Q inserted into the conversation.

"Even some fruitcakes are worthy of attention," the president replied with a wry smile. "The Pope sent one to Melania and me last Christmas, and we loved it."

"Well, this Nostradamus character seems like a different sort of fruitcake," Q shot back. "Did the FBI seize any scrolls when they took him into custody?"

"The French have them. The Bureau got butkis," the president said flatly. "Two special agents were there as observers only. The DGSE swept the place pretty clean from what they were able to tell. President DuPris has since shared with me that DGSE came away from the arrest with a half-dozen parchment scrolls Chastain had handwritten his predictions on, plus a flash drive that was filled with photos and documents. The French have not confirmed this, but our best guess is it contains digital copies of what's on the scrolls."

"So if it's all in custody, why would Chastain return to Sedona?" Doc asked.

"One of the guards Baird had handcuffed around him in Gitmo said Chastain talked about having stashed two more scrolls and a second flash drive as a back-up. It appears that in his twisted mind, he must have them to prove he can foretell the future."

"But why risk being recaptured?" Doc probed. "He just needs to rewrite his predictions."

"That seems to be the catch," the president said. "Chastain apparently wrote the predictions while he was in some sort of trance. He can fully remember them afterward. So the scrolls—and the flash drives—are his only solid connection to his predictions, and his only proof of what he predicted, and when."

"And it all means that much to him?" Q pressed the point. "None of this makes any sense to me, Mr. President."

"Me either!" Doc chimed in. "Especially the part about why the French government is treating him with kid gloves."

"From where we're standing, nothing about Chastain makes any sense, fellas," the president declared. "That's why I've invited French ambassador Andre LeCarre to join us for a briefing when you arrive. Time is not on our side in this, fellas. I'm not about to let Jonah Baird roam around the country at will. And I've given my word to President DuPris that the United States will not interfere with his efforts to bring a French hero to justice.

"Fellas, your team must be ready to move the moment we know where Baird and the Frenchman are headed next," the president said. "So, the briefing will start as soon as you arrive in the Oval Office."

"Understood, Mr. President," Doc replied simply.

"My staff will make certain that Connie and Marsha have all the support they need for a smooth transition out to Camp David," the president pledged. "Please apologize for me for not welcoming them back properly."

"Will do, Mr. President," Doc said.

"Oh, and one more thing before I end the call," the president said. "Be sure that Madeleine comes to the briefing with you."

"Of course, Mr. President," Doc answered with a trace of surprise that he shared with a look at Q, sitting beside him. "See you soon!"

"Indeed! See you soon!" the president responded and ended the call.

Q and Doc exchanged quizzical looks for a moment as the screen returned to black.

"Was that odd, or what?" Q finally asked.

"Definitely," was Doc's only immediate reply.

"So, what do you think?" Q prodded.

"What do you mean, what do I think?" Doc wasn't in the mood to speculate.

"What's the president's sudden interest in Madeleine?" Q asked anyway.

"I don't know, Q," Doc said, a little agitated. "Why didn't you ask him?"

"I'm not going to ask the leader of the free world, who happens to be married, why he wants to see a woman?" Q said as his face grew red.

"Well, you're obviously assuming the worst," Doc now was having fun. "Don't you think the fair thing to do would be to simply ask the man?"

"I don't want to get involved," Q said sharply.

"You see pretty involved to me," Doc said with a chuckle as the two of them headed out to rejoin the rest of the team in the main cabin.

Jenny, Louis, Connie, Marsha, Noah, and Madeleine were caught up in a fast-paced card game and hardly noticed when Doc and Q rejoined them.

"What are you playing?" Q asked.

"Uno!" Jenny said, without looking up for fear of breaking her concentration.

"What?" Q asked again.

"Uno!" everyone yelled.

"It looks like a kid's game," Q told them.

"It's harder than it looks," Louis assured him.

"Play some poker, and I'll join you," Q offered.

"Don't have the cards," Marsha said as drew a card.

"Where'd you get these?" Q asked.

"Portia got 'em for us," Connie replied and took her turn.

"So you're sayin' our billionaire president doesn't have a poker deck on his personal Dreamliner, but he's got a deck of Uno cards," Q stated the facts sarcastically.

"Who knew?" Madeleine added with a giggle.

"Wanna bet the media would have a problem with that if they knew?" Doc asked Q as he settled into a high-back chair near Connie. "Is the game almost over?" he asked no one in particular.

"Uno! I'm about to win," Noah said with a broad smile as he did exactly that.

"You cheated!" Madeleine told him and tossed her cards into the center of the table.

"You always say that when I win," he laughed back at her.

"You don't win when you don't cheat," his wife playfully shot back at him.

"We will be landing in approximately ten minutes, everyone," Marie announced and returned the cards to their box.

Doc made eye contact with Madeleine and Noah as they headed back to their seats.

"Madeleine, the president made a point of asking that you attend the briefing," Doc said.

"Well, of course, Doc," she replied with a slight smile. "Did he say why?"

"It must have something to do with France's involvement in all this," Noah guessed.

"That would be my guess," Doc agreed.

"But I'm a researcher, not a diplomat," Madeleine reasoned. "The president knows that."

"That he does," Doc answered and glanced at Q. "The president knows that and much, much more—which is why I usually just pass along his requests without a lot of questions."

"I'll be interested to learn the reason," Madeleine said thoughtfully.

"That makes two of us," Noah chimed in.

"You can be sure he has a reason," Doc summed up the conversation. "There's a reason for everything the president says and does."

"Sounds like your 'everything happens for a reason' philosophy has a new twist," Q said as he and Doc headed to their seats.

"Does that mean that after all this time around me, you

still have doubts?" Doc asked with a touch of exasperation.

"Oh, I'm sure there's a reason," Q said softly. "I just hope it's one we're all comfortable with, if you know what I mean."

"Take your seat beside Marsha, Mr. Sunshine, and buckle up," Q simply said.

Doc slid into the seat beside Connie and took hold of the hand she had on the armrest nearest him. Then he momentarily got lost in the hypnotic eyes of the love of his life.

"Are Marsha and I going to the White House with the rest of you?" she asked softly.

"I'm afraid not this trip, Beauty," he answered her. "The president has Secret Service waiting for the two of you at Ronald Reagan to take you to Camp David. The plan, as we know it, is for the team to head out immediately following the briefing. But I'll check in before we leave."

"Do you have any idea how long you'll be gone this time, John?" Connie asked earnestly.

"None, Beauty," Doc answered. "Q and I are both determined to end this cat and mouse with Baird once and for all. So we'll be gone as long as there's any chance of that mad man ever being on the loose again."

"He's responsible for the taking of so many innocent

lives," Connie said and squeezed his hand harder than usual. "Please promise me you'll be careful, John. Please."

"I promise, Beauty," Doc assured her sincerely. "And I promise you I'll bring everybody back safely with me too."

"Prepare for landing," Portia announced in the cabin, then took her seat and buckled up.

In the hanger, Doc couldn't help but notice that Madeleine and Noah made a point of climbing into the same SUV as he did. So he was ready for questions from them on the ride to the White House. But none were asked. Instead, the two of them listened intently to his thoughts about the briefing they were headed to, and they seemed to be taking mental notes. That wasn't unusual for Noah. But Madeleine's silence surprised Doc.

As they rolled over the Rochambeau Memorial Bridge into D.C., he stole a glance at her as she stared out at the Potomac River. He recalled their first meeting in the Vatican's Secret Library. She looked much younger then, but the three years since she had added to her allure. Doc recalled his surprise that she was as attractive and brilliant as Jonah Baird had described her when he gave Doc the directions on where to find her.

Therein was another of the many ironies about this adventure. Jonah Baird had arranged for Doc to meet Madeleine in Rome to learn about her groundbreaking research into the whereabouts of the lost treasure of the Knights Templar, which ultimately paved the way for Doc and his team to find it. Doc valued her input but rejected her request to join his team. It was Baird who insisted that Doc accept Madeleine's help in the search. And ultimately, she played a key role in locating the treasure, which had eluded hunters for more than 700 years.

Sadly, the billions of dollars that it brought underwrote the insane plot that Baird hatched to murder writers and other artists around the globe and memorialize the murders in his macabre Forbidden Library. Meanwhile, Doc's share of the treasure—and Madeleine's help finding it—set the team on a course to become a quick-response, unstoppable force for good.

Now, Doc and his team were headed to a White House meeting to discuss how they could bring Baird to justice while avoiding a confrontation between the U.S. and France over Baird's new partner, an AWOL French Foreign Legionnaire who believed he was Nostradamus himself. It was the team's toughest challenge yet. And this time, the President of the United States had specifically asked that Madeleine take part in the meeting. Doc thought it must be connected to her French heritage and her gift for historical research. But it was for a far more important reason.

# 7

## "THE DOZEN"

With all his billions, Baird could afford the best. So he demanded it from his Guardian army, just as he demanded their selfless loyalty. Guardians traded their souls for the life Baird's money provided. He fed them, clothed them, housed them, and paid them well to serve him with unquestioning loyalty in every thought and action. And they did just that.

The army had grown to more than 400 since Baird formed it nearly three years earlier to help him establish and guard his "Forbidden Library." He now wasn't exactly sure how many Guardians there were. The number was almost meaningless since there were more of them with almost every passing day. Guardians recruited and trained new recruits, and the army grew while Baird planned his evil purposes.

Though some, like the two pilots in Texas, had run-ins with state, county, or local law enforcement, there was really only one unknown quantity that stood between Baird and his vicious objectives: "The Dozen"—Doc and his team vexed the mad man at every major turn of his grand plan for his Forbidden Library. Baird was certain that, if not for them, the world would still be none the wiser regarding his master plan to murder writers and artists around the world and pass them off as suicides. If not for Doc and his team, the original Forbidden Library in Washington, D.C., would still exist and would likely be almost filled with the final, offensive works of his victims.

Instead, Baird now had to start all over. But Baird was determined that his plan would not be denied. His Forbidden Library would soon be a reality once again, and the murders required to fill its shelves would resume. While whittling away the time in solitary confinement, Baird eventually realized Doc and his team had unwittingly done him a favor.

Because of them, the world now knew what at first appeared to be tragic suicides were really murders. So that part of his plan was scuttled, and Baird could simply order Guardians to murder creative types whose work offended him. They were adept at doing that just about anywhere in the world. They were equally skilled at bringing Baird the mementos he designated from the homes of his victims, which he proudly displayed along with samples of the offending works. Baird was eager and excited to begin that macabre labor of love again.

But Chastain was focused on retrieving the one

remaining digital copy of his scrolls he'd hidden before he was captured in his Sedona hideout by the DGSE. He was, however, also flattered that Baird wanted printed copies of the scrolls for his Forbidden Library. But Chastain didn't have to worry that Baird would have him murdered. Baird wasn't offended by the scrolls; they excited him. This was an unexpected twist in Baird's vision for his Forbidden Library, and he loved it. Best of all, the world had no idea what catastrophic event was foretold on one of the scrolls. Even Doc's team had no clue.

"Good to see you again, Captain Holiday!" Marine Sergeant Walters said as he opened the SUV's rear door and saluted Doc. "Welcome back to the White House, sir!"

"It's good to see you again too, Sergeant Walters," Doc said as he returned the salute and stepped out of the Suburban, onto the brick pavers at the north entrance.

"What's the president's mood today, Sergeant?" Doc asked as the two of them led the team on a brisk walk along the west wing to the Oval Office.

"A bit edgy compared to his usual cool," the sergeant replied. "But, he's smiling as always."

"I'll do my best to keep him that way," Doc said softly.

"I know you will, sir. Good luck," the sergeant said and saluted again as he left Doc and the team in the reception area just outside the Oval Office.

When Camilla Renfro, President Prescott's secretary, ushered the team into the Oval Office, Doc had Madeleine and Noah on either side of him. Q, Jenny, and Louis followed them in. Doc had been in the room a number of times during his brief time with the Secret Service. But the rest of his team, like all first-time visitors to the office, were quieted by the feeling of history and power within its walls. The effect always ensured the president was the first to speak.

"Welcome!" the president said, standing in front of the resolute desk with open arms.

"Hello, Mr. President!" Doc said enthusiastically, and the others chimed in as well.

"You're right on time," President Prescott said. "We have several minutes to speak freely before French Ambassador LeCarre arrives. So if you have tough questions for me, now's the time to ask them. Fire away!"

"Have you learned any more about Baird and the Frenchmen's plans since we spoke aboard your plane?" Doc asked.

"Well, we're more certain they're headed to Sedona," the president said. "Beyond that, your guess is a good as ours."

"Have you already got people on the ground there?" Q asked.

"We've alerted local authorities, of course," the president replied, "and Homeland Security and the FBI are on the perimeter in case you need them. But you six— whom I refer to only as 'the Dozen,' are the point of the spear on bringing Baird back.

"Why 'the Dozen'?" Doc asked.

"Because any one of you is equal to at least two of any others in the world who do what you do," the president said fondly. "I've always been sincere in my admiration and gratitude for your individual and collective roles in keeping our nation safe and secure. Somehow, I've been blessed with what I am sure are the six absolute best our nation has. I have no other way of explaining your successful completion of each of the missions I've given to you so far.

"What's more, and every bit as important, you're extraordinary efforts remain known only to a select few other Americans who have needed to know about you and what it is you do on behalf of our nation. Given the extreme importance of the tasks I've set before you, and the potential international implications if you had failed, you're unsung heroics are without a doubt among the most incredible aspects behind the legacy I will eventually leave as president. Yet no one knows your names… and most incredibly, you're all okay with that. Which is why this man, this President of the United States, so fondly—and proudly—calls you 'the Dozen.'"

"Did you rehearse that?" Q asked, to lighten the mood and break the silence the president's unexpected and very high praise had brought to the room.

"Just ignore him, please, Mr. President," Doc sighed while the others all laughed.

"I can tell you I've fallen asleep thinking about it a number of times," the president said.

"Mr. President," Camilla's pleasant voice came softly over the intercom, "Ambassador LeCarre is approaching. He's brought a French military officer along with him."

"Thanks, Camilla," the president replied.

"Perfect timing once again!" President Prescott said cheerfully. "Doc, I'd appreciate you and Madeleine staying for this meeting, please," the president said as Camilla surprised the group by opening a door on the opposite side of the Oval Office to show Q and the others out.

"Do you have a twin, or are you just very good at what you do?" Q asked as a compliment in his trademark flippant way.

"I assure you, Q, there's not another like her," the president took the opportunity to say as the team exited the office.

"I've directed my staff to make sure they have a terrific lunch in the White House Mess," the president said. "Now, let's see what Ambassador LeCarre has for us, shall we?"

Doc could only smile and silently wonder at the way

Camilla so quickly and gracefully ushered the ambassador and officer into the office via the door back on the side of the room she'd used to show the team in. He guessed he'd never know just how she so expertly choreographed entries and exits via one door or the other. It was just one more example of the "magic" that happens in the world's most amazing and powerful house.

"Alexandre?!" Madeleine exclaimed as the strapping French Foreign Legionnaire stepped into the office.

"Madeleine Marie!" was his only reply as he crossed the room in just two steps and swept her up his arms.

"When I read the advance file on Sergeant Bellarose, I thought it would be nice to give you two a chance to see each other, Madeleine," the president chuckled. "So, I asked Doc to make sure you came."

"My long-lost brother!" Madeleine squealed. "Whom, by the way, I haven't heard from in the past six years."

"I meant to write," the handsome, 6'3" officer said as he slipped the beret off his head. "I just didn't know what to say."

"Forgive me," Madeleine said and regained her composure. "There's time enough for this later."

"It's okay, really," the president said with a smile. "It's always nice to see people so happy. That's not guaranteed in this room."

Camilla quietly slipped into the room almost unnoticed

and took a seat just behind Doc and Madeleine, with a steno pad and pen in hand. She began writing immediately, and Doc wondered how much of her being there was merely a distraction to help those in the room forget that every word uttered was being captured by a dozen or more microphones located strategically about the Oval Office.

"But forgive me Ambassador LeCarre and Lieutenant Colonel of France's 2nd Foreign Parachute Regimen Alexandre Rafael Bellarose," the president said, congenially. "It's my pleasure to introduce you to retired Navy Captain John Henry Holiday and a member of his support staff, Ms. Madeleine Allaman. I hope you don't mind, but I asked them to join us because they will assist in the recapture of Jonah Baird, who was last seen in the company of your missing Legionnaire Gabriel Chastain, and I want to ensure they understand the status and sensitivity of the situation at hand."

"I'm glad you did, Mr. President," the ambassador said. "Recent events have put France in the difficult position of preserving Legionnaire Chastain's well-deserved legacy of service and honor, while also ensuring the safety of the public at large. His extraordinary ability to evade our best efforts to capture and contain him could severely tarnish that legacy if the French people were to learn of his recent misadventures."

*What Q would do with a statement like that!* Doc thought to himself.

"I understand he earned the Legion of Honor, your

country's highest military honor," Doc said to the ambassador. "He is an exceptional soldier and man, indeed."

"He did," the ambassador confirmed. "As did the Legionnaire beside me, when fast, unselfish actions by both of them saved an entire regiment during the Battle of Tikrit," the ambassador proudly stated and gently poked Madeleine's brother with an elbow.

"Our surveillance planes are tracking Chastain and Baird as we speak," the president said. "They're still aboard a small prop plane over central Texas, with a heading that will take them over Sedona in a few hours. Our intelligence tells us they'll likely spend some time in the Sedona area, where we believe Legionnaire Chastain stashed digital copies of his scrolls that supposedly predict future events. Mr. Ambassador, what can you tell us about the scrolls? I believe your DGSE has a number of them in custody. Is that correct?"

"It is," the ambassador said. "And French intelligence has learned important things from them. First, they do appear to be predictions rather than mere guesses about the future. Second,

though, it's not always the case, a number of his predictions are extremely detailed. Third, he foretold a number of recent events with roughly 90 percent accuracy. And most intriguing, his more recent predictions are his most accurate, by roughly 97 percent."

"So how exactly does he do it?" the president leaned in and asked.

Madeleine and Doc leaned into the conversation at this point as well. They both listened intently and didn't make a sound. It wasn't lost on them that Madeliene's brother hadn't uttered a word since arriving either.

"We do not have a clue!" the ambassador said emphatically, as though the jackpot question had just been asked. "We *do know* that he sustained a traumatic brain injury in Tikrit, which he miraculously survived. He was in a coma and near death for ten months. But then he suddenly regained consciousness and appeared not to have suffered any lasting effects from his injuries. There's no explaining it, Mr. President. Nor can we explain the abilities he now appears to possess. According to what we know, he foresees events while in a kind of trance, then writes them down when he awakens. It seems he often cannot recall them shortly afterward."

"That's an amazing story, Ambassador LeCarre," the president said. "Did he begin doing this during, or soon after, his recovery?"

"During," the ambassador said. "One day in the hospital, he simply asked for paper and a pen and began writing. The nurses thought it was simply a good thing for him to do and might aid in his recovery. But not long afterward, one of his nurses happened to read a page as it lay beside him while he slept. What she read described a fire that would begin in the hospital's kitchen a week later. She thought it was merely fanciful fiction writing and thought nothing more of it until the fire actually occurred and progressed through two other sections of the hospital's basement, just as Legionnaire Chastain had foretold in his writing."

"And, of course, this was all thoroughly investigated by fire and police officials?" the president asked for the record.

"Most thoroughly," the ambassador replied. "Meanwhile, he foretold a number of other large and small events that soon occurred with varying degrees of accuracy. Eventually, he was released from the hospital and lived quietly in a small apartment for the next year.

"Then one day he simply walked into a local office of the municipal police and claimed an assassination attempt would soon be made on President DuPris. It was during that visit to the local police that he first claimed he is Nostradamus and became uncharacteristically belligerent. The bizarre episode brought him to the attention of the DGSE, who foiled the assassination plot, thanks to the details in one of his scrolls. Shortly afterward, Legionnaire Chastain went AWOL from his unit. When the DGSE located him, they decided to keep him under close surveillance rather than arrest him in the hope of learning more about his behavior and associates."

"So why did he come to the U.S.?" the president finally asked.

"It appears he was invited by your fugitive, Jonah Baird," the ambassador answered. "DGSE tells us your Mr. Baird learned of Legionnaire Chastain's scrolls and asked to meet with him to discuss the possibility of adding them to something Mr. Baird calls his Forbidden Library.

"By the time Legionnaire Chastain arrive in Arizona, your Mr. Baird had been captured and sent to Guantanamo. While in Sedona, our AWOL Legionnaire let it slip to an informant that he planned to help Mr. Baird escape. One late night last week, the DGSE did a routine search of his apartment while he was enjoying the Sedona nightlife and discovered several handwritten scrolls and flash drive back-ups. One of the scrolls contains a detailed foretelling of a successful assassination of President DuPris during his planned visit here in Washington next month. That's when they took him into custody, and President DuPris asked Secretary of State McDonnaly to hold him temporarily at your Guantanamo Detention Center.

"My government was preparing to return him to France when he escaped with your Mr. Baird," the ambassador said. "It was disturbing to learn Legionnaire Chastain assaulted and threatened to kill one of his guards during the escape. That's quite unlike the hero we know. He obviously will require extensive medical and psychological support. Getting him back home will just as obviously require more than we had originally planned. So I'm very pleased and grateful to tell you that Lieutenant Colonel Bellarose volunteered to ensure his fellow

Medal of Honor recipient gets back to France safe and sound."

"I know Captain Holiday will appreciate having his many skills to call upon in bringing these two men back where they belong," President Prescott said. "And of course, Madeleine will no doubt enjoy some unexpected time with her brother. But there's one more thing we must discuss before they head to their plane."

"What might that be?" the ambassador asked and finally leaned in.

The President rose from his chair and handed everyone a file marked "Top Secret."

"As you will see on page three, under 'Unexplained Phenomena,' Legionnaire Chastain put on quite a show during the brief time he spent as our guest at Gitmo," the president said. "I regret that those files must remain in this office."

"Has this been verified?" the ambassador gasped as he read the file.

"It has…twice," the president responded. "Is there anything in his medical records you haven't shared with us that would account for this?"

"Not hardly," the ambassador said, as he took off his glasses and rubbed his eyes. "It appears our Legionnaire is a man of *many more* talents than we realized."

He put a hand on the Bellarose's arm and asked, "Are you still up for this Colonel?"

"More than ever, Mr. Ambassador!" the paratrooper replied enthusiastically. "It appears this will be even more interesting than I imagined!"

"Mr. Ambassador, you're welcome to join me in the Situation Room for a live feed on the progress of your Legionnaire's plane," the president said as he ended the meeting. "Doc, Madeleine, Colonel Bellarose, the live feed has been patched to the plane that's waiting for you."

# 8

## "MYSTERIES OF THE SUN AND SOUL"

Q, Jenny, Louis, and Noah were already waiting in the three hulking, black Suburbans idling at the north entrance of the White House when Doc led Madeleine and her brother outside. Two were plenty, so Doc wondered why there were three but wrote it off as extra security.

"Ready when you are!" Q quipped through his open window as the trio approached.

"Step out and mind your manners everyone," Doc announced as two Marines opened the SUVs' doors. "Jenny, Louis, Noah, and Q, I am thrilled to introduce you to Madeleine's big brother, Lieutenant-Colonel Alexandre Rafael Bellarose of France's 2nd Foreign Parachute Regiment, whose mission it is to return the mysterious Legionnaire 1e Classe Gabriel Chastain, also known as Nostradamus, to France at the earliest possible moment."

"Just call me 'Rafe,' if you please," the handsome, strapping Legionnaire said with a captivating smile. "And Captain, if you please, refer to Legionnaire 1e Classe Gabriel Chastain by that name only. I'm certain the Legionnaire I know is not willingly or willfully acting as the man you refer to as Nostradamus. I fought beside him for nearly three years. I am also confident that I would be dead today if he had been on my left instead of on my right his last day in Tikrit. Still, while bleeding and barely breathing, he helped me save nearly every man in our regiment while the enemy bombarded us with mortars for a solid hour. He is not a make-believe 16th-century madman. He is a courageous 21st-century warrior."

"So noted!" Doc replied. "Please forgive the lapse, Colonel Bellarose. Perhaps we've run our ship a little too loose for too long. And please, just call me Doc."

"No problem, Doc," Rafe assured him. "Just go light on the 'Nostradamus' thing."

The Suburbans ran with their blue lights flashing, so the ride to Joint Base Andrews took less than 20 minutes. When the team arrived, they were surprised when the SUVs pulled up to a huge C-130 Hercules. Even with its noise suppression system engaged, they could feel the rumble of the plane's four massive Rolls Royce AE2100D3 turboprop engines through their feet when they stepped out onto the tarmac.

"Well, they'll sure see us comin'," Q wisecracked.

"It seems like a lot more plane than we need," Madeleine added.

"It's perfect," Rafe said softly with another of his charming smiles.

The loading crew opened the back doors of the SUVs. From the first two vehicles, they unloaded two weapons chests Doc brought from Montana. They were roughly six feet by three feet by three feet and weighed roughly 200 pounds each. The third vehicle held two of Rafe's weapons chests. Each measured eight feet by three feet by three feet and weighed about 400 pounds. Doc didn't want to lug so much armor around but then thought better of challenging "the French way" of doing things.

Minutes later, the team was in the air headed west. Doc knew the plane's cruising speed far exceeded its official 360 miles per hour. So he wasn't surprised when the pilot announced an ETA of 1400 hours Mountain Standard Time.

"We'll have plenty of daylight when we get there," he told the team. "That's just three hours from now. So get your rest now, 'cause all hell's going to break loose when we land."

As the team settled in, Doc quietly took Madeleine aside.

"You probably should use some of this time to talk with your brother," he told her. "I'm not at all certain when you're next chance will be for a while."

"Thanks for that, Doc," she said. "I'll try. But we haven't communicated for years. So I'm not expecting a lot."

"Get what you can, Madeleine," he told her. "If anyone can pull information out of people, it's you. Whenever you're ready, I need to hear what you're thinking about Chastain."

Madeleine found her brother sitting alone and silent. So she dropped into the seat facing his and put her foot up on his seat in a casual way. But it was a strategic move that subliminally and actually made it more difficult for her brother to easily exit the seat.

"I've missed you terribly, Alexandre," she told him softly and placed her hand over his on the arm of his seat. "Sorry if I put you on the spot back in D.C., but I had no clue you were going to walk into the room. I hope you can understand how surprised and off my game I was."

"I understand completely, Madeleine," Rafe told her. "I had very little notice that I was going to be a part of this search. And Ambassador LeCarre did not tell me you were part of the team until I arrived in D.C. early this morning. I think no one really put two and two together until the last minute. It might have happened sooner if you were using your maiden name. When did you get married?"

"Nearly two years ago, now," she answered.

"Who's the lucky guy, and when do I meet him?" Rafe asked.

"Noah Allaman," she told him. "That's him right over there. Come on, I'll introduce you. He's anxious to meet you."

"Sweetheart, this is Alexandre, the big brother I've told you about," Madeleine told her husband. "Guess it's pretty obvious by now that I didn't tell you everything. But I would have…if I had known about it! Alexandre, this is my wonderful husband, Noah. I couldn't tell you everything about him in a million years!"

"I'm very pleased to finally meet you, Alexandre," Noah said as he rose and shook Rafe's hand.

"I'm pleased to meet you as well, Noah. And call me Rafe, please," Rafe replied. "Only my sister and strangers call me Alexandre."

"So I guess I'm still in the 'guest' category," Madeleine shot back for spite.

"Not as far as I'm concerned," Rafe assured her. "But that's up to you now."

"I'll leave you two here to get to know one another," Madeleine said. "I've got to give Doc a bit of a history lesson. And Rafe…I'm very glad you're here."

"That makes two of us, Sis," the imposing Legionnaire replied.

"Your brother makes quite an impressive entrance with

that bright red beret, the gold paratrooper wings, and all those hard-earned ribbons," Doc said when Madeleine sat beside him.

"I know!" she sighed. "It all causes a disconnect when I try to think of him as the big brother with a bad haircut who used to walk me to school."

"If we can stay in our separate lanes regarding objectives and tactics, I believe he's going to make us all happy we have him along on this mission," Doc said. "So back to work. What can you tell me about the real Nostradamus and why Chastain might claim to be him?"

"Well, the comparison's not perfect," Madeleine began, "I guess you could say Michel de Nostredame, is the French equivalent of America's Edgar Cayse. Nostradamus is the Latinized version of his name. He died in 1566, and his books of supposedly prophetic poems have virtually never been out of print since he published them. He and his poems remain popular around the world. But to the best of my knowledge, Chastain's the first to claim to be him."

"Do you believe the real Nostradamus foretold the future?" Doc asked her earnestly.

"No," she said. "But I'm in the minority. There is another researcher, Peter Lemesurier, who has studied Nostradamus's writings extensively and believes he practiced bibliomancy."

"What?!" Doc asked in confusion.

"Bibliomancy," she repeated. "It's a prediction technique that dates back to biblical times, based simply on the belief that history repeats itself. Lemesurier claims that Nostradamus was neither an astrologer nor a seer, but merely selected ancient accounts of past events from older sources at random. Then he used astrological calculations to project the likelihood the events would recur in the future. According to Lemesurier, one of the major sources Nostradamus used for his most famous work, *The Prophecies*, was the *Mirabilis liber* of 1522, an anthology of prophecies from well-known seers of the time."

"This is way over my head," Doc confessed. "Did he or didn't he predict the future?"

"I'm not saying he did or didn't, Doc," she answered. "I'm saying many people believe he did, but many don't. For me, the real test is that no one's been able to read his books and gain any meaningful knowledge about a future event *before* it actually occurs. So I wasn't surprised that Ambassador LeCarre's report doesn't conclusively say French intelligence believes Chastain has foretold the future. All they're willing to say about the scrolls is they contain information about events that may or may not happen. In fact, it sounds to me like they're more worried he's plotting something they're trying to keep from happening. That has nothing to do with prophecy."

"That's exactly where I'm at with this," Doc agreed.

"Ultimately, what matters about Chastain is that your brother safely returns him to France, and we figure out what to do about the unexplained phenomena we read on page three of the file the President shared with us."

"Still, we need to be mindful of the influence Chastain is no doubt having on Baird," Madeleine told Doc. "Whether or not Baird believes Chastain's claims, you can bet he's got plans to use him and his scrolls any way he can. In that respect, history is indeed kind of repeating itself."

"What do you mean?" Doc asked.

"In September 1939," Madeleine explained, "shortly after Germany invaded Poland, Magda Goebbels, the wife of Hitler's propaganda minister, Joseph Goebbels, stumbled upon a passage in a book entitled *Mysteries of the Sun and Soul,* in which one of Nostradamus's quatrains appeared to predict that crises would develop in England and Poland in 1939. Good propaganda minister that he was, Goebbels ordered that reference be used in a brochure to explain to those living in neutral countries that a Nazi victory was inevitable…just as Nostradamus had supposedly predicted centuries earlier."

"Well, what little we know about Baird's Guardians tells me they'll be easy enough to persuade that Chastain is really Nostradamus and that he can help them with their international murder spree," Doc surmised.

"But don't be too quick to blow off the possibility that

he *really can* foresee the future, Doc," Madeleine warned. "He *did* predict his escape from Gitmo with Baird before he even knew they'd be locked up together there. If he knows what's coming next, any telekinetic powers he may have are even more dangerous. I don't know how we can overcome an enemy who knows our every move before we make it…especially if he can counter our best moves without moving a muscle."

"Do me a favor and don't talk about this with Q," Doc sighed. "He'd have a field day messing with my mind. In the meantime, I guess we'll find out soon enough whether Chastain can really see the future. We'll have a good idea if we find Guardians ready and waiting for us in Sedona. Speaking of Sedona, let's bring everyone together now and get them up to speed."

Doc and Madeleine had their thoughts about the mission reinforced when Rafe shared his thoughts at the end of the briefing.

"Make no mistake," Rafe said, "my primary mission is to secure Legionnaire Chastain and safely return him to France, so he can receive the help and support he deserves as a hero. But our joint mission is to have each other's backs when we engage him and the mad man he has with him. If Chastain now has even half the mind power U.S. intelligence reports, we are about to face the most unbelievable opposition of our careers…and our very lives will depend upon how well we meet the challenge as a team. So, while my primary mission remains to secure Chastain, I'm all in with your team personally.

You have the full support of every skill and resource I've brought with me. I promise you that."

"I love this guy," Doc told Madeleine softly.

"Me too!" she replied.

Doc was glad when Q settled into a nearby chair, but he braced for what he could only guess was coming.

"Madeleine," Q chuckled with a devilish grin, "you need to tell your brother about the 700-year-old Templar Knight we ran up against in Israel."

"I don't think he's ready for that...or for you," Madeleine shot back with a devilish grin of her own.

"Speaking of being ready, Doc—is this Nostradamus character for real, or not?" Q asked.

Doc paused long enough to take a deep breath and measure his answer.

"Maybe," he said simply.

"So you're saying Chastain really can do some supernatural things, both mentally and physically?" Q probed for details Doc hadn't shared during the briefing.

"Maybe," Doc said again.

"Do you really think we can corral him and Baird with such big 'maybes'?" Q asked anxiously.

"Maybe," Doc sighed.

"Why do you talk like an old-fashioned, cynical

cowboy, Q?" Madeleine asked in the hope of steering the conversation away from the unknown. "We have no reason to doubt the report from the Guantanamo commander. It appears Chastain's done some things that can't be easily explained. But we've encountered the unexplainable before, and it hasn't stopped us yet."

"Well said, Madeleine," Doc added.

"Indeed!" Rafe interjected as he joined the conversation. "Are you at liberty to provide any examples?"

"We once faced off with a 700-year-old Templar Knight," Q said whimsically.

Madeleine shot Q a frustrated look.

"I thought we agreed not to bring that up?" Madeleine sighed.

"Well, is your brother a member of the team or not?" Q asked with a shrug.

"Yeah, Madeleine," Rafe chided her. "Am I a member or not?"

"You are," Doc stated emphatically. "And we're lucky to have you! So fill him in, Madeleine. Then bring him into the screening room they rigged for us just behind the cockpit. I just got a text from the president, and he's got an update for us."

Madeleine and Rafe joined Doc and Q in the screening room and donned headphones just as President Prescott began detailing the Sommerville Lake incident that had just unfolded.

"Do you know for certain whether Baird and Chastain were on either of the planes?" Doc asked the president.

"The two Texas Park and Wildlife Wardens, Justin Markham and Carlos Riaz, didn't see them. But we found the original light plane they used to escape in South Florida, and we suspected they boarded a second plane for the long haul to Arizona. If so, they might have needed to refuel—or transfer to a third plane—and the Dallas area is a likely place for that."

"Then it's a good bet they were on board the plane that got away," Rafe said confidently. "I believe they arrived aboard the first plane that flew in from the east and slipped aboard the second plane before it took off. I served with Chastain for three years, and I can assure you that the wardens would never have seen him unless he wanted them to."

"If you're right, they're going to be in Arizona in about an hour," the president said.

"And their traveling by seaplane?" Rafe asked.

"The wardens looked the plane up online, and it's a newly developed personal craft called an AirFish 8. It's exclusively a watercraft," the president answered.

"Can you pull up a map of Arizona on this screen, Mr. President?" Rafe asked.

In a moment, Arizona filled the screen.

"Where's Sedona?" Rafe asked.

Doc pointed it out for him, and Rafe scanned the surrounding area for bodies of water.

"They'll likely put down right here, on Lake Pleasant," he said. "That'll put them less than a couple hours' drive from Sedona."

"That's about the time you'll be over that area," the president told them.

"We'll land at Luke Air Force Base, outside Phoenix and be in Sedona by midafternoon," Doc calculated.

"I'll be going in under my own power," Rafe said. "So I should arrive shortly after they do. But don't worry. I won't make a move on them until you all get there."

"You'll get there *two hours before us?*" Q asked in bewilderment. "How?"

"Please enlighten us," Doc said.

"I brought a wingsuit," Rafe said matter-of-factly.

"You brought a wingsuit?!" Doc echoed.

"I did," Rafe answered simply.

"Why would you bring a wingsuit?" Doc asked in amazement.

"Why wouldn't I?" Rafe answered simply. "It goes with

me everywhere. It's a huge time saver on missions like this, and time is of the utmost importance."

"Oh, of the utmost, for sure," Q said in his unique way.

"So what do you plan to do with all the time you'll save, Colonel?" the president asked.

"Well, right now, we have no idea where Chastain will hide," Rafe said. "Show me the terrain around Sedona, and I suspect I can find him. He favors unique wilderness settings."

"Sounds good!" the president answered. "I'll get you patched into the Situation Room, and they'll have someone provide you with the info you need. Nice work, Colonel!"

"Thank you, Mr. President," Rafe answered.

"What work?" Q whispered to Doc. "So far, he's all talk."

"Why Q, you sound jealous," Doc whispered back.

"I don't like being outmaneuvered," Q said quietly. "Let alone out-equipped."

"I'll gladly buy you a wingsuit," Doc offered wryly.

"That's not funny," Q grumbled softly.

"It would be funny just to see you in one," Doc replied while stifling a laugh.

A live satellite image of the Sedona area suddenly appeared on the screen.

"Stand by for encrypted communication," a mechanical voice announced.

"My word, that's rough, desolate terrain!" Rafe said aloud.

"Happy wingsuiting!" Q replied sarcastically.

## 9

### DEVIL'S BRIDGE

"Madeleine, please ask Noah, Jenny, and Louis to come in here for this," Doc requested. "We're about three and a half hours away from needing to know all we can about Sedona."

"Except for your brother, of course," Q interjected. "He'll fly in under his own power a couple of hours ahead of us."

"I have a buddy harness," Rafe said with a smile. "Would you like to join me, Q?"

"Um…no. Thanks, but no thanks." Q said emphatically. "I prefer to be indoors when I'm in the air."

"I'd love to try it sometime, Alexandre," Madeleine said. "But I'm not quite ready."

"I understand," Rafe said. "It takes some getting used to."

"Somehow, I just don't think I could ever get used to jumping out of an airplane," Q said.

Doc just smiled at Q's rare admission of fear.

"You're looking at a live satellite view of the area surrounding Sedona, Arizona," a voice said over the satellite connection.

"What's that stone arch in the center of the picture?" Rafe asked.

"Devil's Bridge. It's naturally eroded sandstone, roughly 100 feet high with a span of about 135 feet, and is just 12 feet across at its narrowest point. It's less than a half-hour's drive north of Sedona...but Apollo astronauts who trained in the area say it resembles the far side of the moon. The arch is normally a popular tourist attraction. However, we've cordoned the area off for you with the story that you're with the Army Corps of Engineers, inspecting the structure and surroundings to check their stability and safety. You have appropriately marked vehicles ready and waiting for at Luke Air Force Base, about a two-hour drive from Sedona—unless you run into rush hour traffic."

"Boy, I sure hate to see you miss out on experiencing rush hour traffic, Rafe," Q said.

Rafe ignored Q's chiding and pulled a small note pad and a short pencil from his shirt pocket to jot down the key things he needed to know.

"What's that large rock feature roughly 200 yards southeast of the bridge?" he asked.

"Devil's Doorknob," the voice replied.

"The devil has a doorknob?" Q asked, but no one answered.

"What are the coordinates of the bridge?" he asked.

"Latitude: 34° 54' 5.688" North; Longitude: 111° 48' 40.6152" West," the voice said.

"What's the weather there today?" Rafe asked.

"Sunny, eighty-nine degrees Fahrenheit, 31.7 degrees Celsius," the voice said.

"Wind?" Rafe asked.

"Out of the southeast at 13 miles per hour," the voice said.

"Any change forecast for the next hour?" Rafe asked as he jotted.

"None," the voice said.

"You're really going to do this, aren't you?" Q asked the spit and polish Legionnaire.

"I am," Rafe replied firmly as he exited the briefing room. "Time to begin getting ready. Are you sure you won't join me, Q?" he asked once again to poke at Q just a bit more.

"I'm positive," Q said with a wave of his hand. "Maybe next time."

"I'll hold you to that," Rafe teased him just once more.

"Sounds good!" Q said out loud. "But it'll never happen," he whispered.

Rafe pulled a camo wingsuit from one of his two weapons lockers and stretched it out on the floor of the plane to inspect it. As he pulled his helmet out and examined the visor closely, Doc casually approached him with questions he had to have answers to.

"What's your plan, soldier?" Doc asked while Rafe continued to examine the helmet.

"The pilot will open the rear bay door in approximately 30 minutes, and I'll launch out, headed to the coordinates. I'll have approximately 15 minutes to surveil the target area from the air before touching down. Hopefully, I'll have a fix on their hiding place by that time, and I can stake it out and watch for any activity until you all arrive."

"Why are you so sure he's down there?" Doc probed, concerned about a wild goose chase.

"That Legionnaire's one weakness is that he's a creature of habit," Rafe answered. "In spite of all his training and experience, he consciously or subconsciously gravitates to the familiar. For those who know him, it can provide a strategic advantage—and no one knows him like I do."

"What's so familiar about Devil's Bridge?" Doc asked in surprise. "Has he been to America before?"

"Not at all," Rafe answered. "But he was born in Cahors, France, in a small house his father built almost literally in the shadow of 'Pont Valentre'—more popularly known as 'the Devil's Bridge.' During our time serving together, he almost obsessively had me take his picture with each of Europe's other nine Devil's Bridges in the background."

"There are ten Devil's Bridges in Europe?" Doc asked incredulously.

"France, Portugal, Spain, England, Wales, Austria, Bulgaria, Germany, Switzerland, and Italy—but all those are manmade," Rafe recited in rapid-fire, as though he'd done it several times before. "As soon as I learned of the one in Sedona, I had no doubt where to look for him."

"And you'll radio it in if you find him before we arrive?" Doc had to ask.

"Don't worry, Doc," Rafe replied with a slight smile. "I'll radio it in and sit tight. I have no desire or intention of engaging your Mr. Baird in your absence."

"Do you have your own radio, or do you need one?" Doc asked.

"I have one in my helmet," Rafe told him. "It's linked by satellite to my country's embassy in D.C., and President Prescott also arranged for it to be linked to his Situation

Room as well as your team's radios. We'll be in continuous contact from the moment I step off the open bay door—which will happen in approximately 20 minutes. Now, if you'll excuse me, I must complete my safety check before suiting up," Rafe said, glancing at his watch.

"You bet!" Doc said, hiding his pique that the president had once again failed to tell him everything about a mission.

The battle-tested former SEAL tried to console himself with the possibility that the President might sometimes overlook a detail during briefings—or perhaps simply *assume* that he would discover all he needs to know one way or another. But Doc found no comfort in the thought because he was certain President Prescott *never* overlooked important details.

Doc was surprised when the plane began to climb. Doc thought that must be another detail the president hadn't told him. So he returned to Rafe, who was zipping up his wingsuit.

"What altitude will you launch at?" he asked.

"25,000 feet," Rafe replied matter-of-factly.

"Why so high?" Doc blurted out.

"I don't want my friend to see me coming—if he hasn't already," Rafe said with a raised eyebrow. "If he does, I want to be traveling too fast to be a target."

"Roger that!" Doc blurted out. "How fast will you be flying?"

"I'll slow to about 70 miles per hour near the ground," Rafe told him.

"Really!" Doc barked. "You'll be flying that fast without making a sound?!"

"Without making a sound," Rafe confirmed.

"At this altitude, you'll need oxygen."

"Got it!" Rafe simply said.

"Of course he does, you idiot!" Doc scolded himself silently as he watched the muscular Legionnaire finish zipping into the wingsuit and secure his helmet and visor.

Atop the visor, where civilian wingsuiters typically mount a video camera, Rafe locked on an exotic-looking, holstered automatic handgun.

"That's one I've never seen before," he said.

"It's brand new," Rafe said. "And you didn't see it. It's France's handheld prototype of your country's PHASR rifle. Hopefully, you won't see it in action on the ground —and I'll have to give you a personal demonstration when the mission's over."

"Roger that!" Doc said in agreement. "Good luck, be careful, and Godspeed, Colonel," Doc told the newest member of the team.

"As you say in your Navy, Aye, Aye, Captain," Rafe replied.

The team gathered around to take in the sight of the wingsuited Legionnaire as he turned on his oxygen and headed to the bay door. Madeleine impulsively hugged him tight and held his glance for just a moment.

"Please don't take any foolish chances, Alexandre," she told him and stepped back as the bay door began to fall open, revealing a bright, cloudless sky.

"That was an odd thing to say to a guy who's about to jump out of an airplane," Q told her.

"Not when that guy's your big brother!" she shot right back.

Rafe pressed a button on his watch, and the pilot opened the plane's bay door.

"See you in a couple of hours!" Doc shouted as Rafe stepped to the very edge of the bay door, turned around and saluted the team, then fell back into the deep blue abyss and was gone in an instant.

Rafe fell away from the big C130 at more than 50 miles per hour. He held his legs together and kept his arms tight to his sides to accelerate to more than 100 miles per hour. He reveled in the exhilaration of rocketing through the air almost silently while he counted out 30 seconds. Then he spread his arms and legs in the customary spread-eagle position and watched the heads-up display of speed, altitude, direction, and coordinates inside his dark-tinted visor.

The bold Legionnaire controlled his direction and rate of descent with slight movements of his legs, hips, and shoulders. The strenuous process required maximum fitness, concentration, and stamina—and of course, nerves of steel. As he'd estimated, his cruising speed slowed to 81 miles per hour about 900 feet above the ground, and he skimmed just feet above the jagged ridges and along the rock faces of the mountains surrounding Devil's Bridge. The bright afternoon sun made it relatively easy for Rafe to spot what appeared to be excavation debris near a sandstone outcrop in a well-hidden gorge about a quarter-mile south of Devil's Bridge.

*I've found you, Gabriel,* Rafe thought. *Someone else must have excavated your hiding place. You would never leave telltale debris.*

Rafe navigated out of the gorge to a spot near the Devil's Bridge trailhead and opened his parachute. On the ground, he draped the silk chute over three Saguaros, unzipped his wingsuit, but left it on and radioed the news that he'd found the excavation.

"That's good to hear!" the voice from the Situation Room said. "You *do* have a way of making a very impressive entrance, Colonel."

"You can see me?" Rafe asked.

"We can see your chute," the voice told him. "We also

see an open vehicle approaching your position about two kilometers to the south."

"I thought this area was closed," Rafe said. "Can you see how many are in it?"

"Negative," the voice said. "They're likely part of the detail that cordoned the area off and are just checking you out because they didn't expect you to arrive quite the way you did."

"But be on your guard," Doc said. "They could also be some of Baird's Guardians."

"We'll find out soon enough," Rafe answered. "I can see the dust they're kicking up. They'll be here in a couple of minutes. Stand by."

"Roger that," the voice said.

"Rafe, you got this?" Doc asked over the radio.

"Absolutely," Rafe replied as he moved his weapon from his helmet to his belt and put on his special dark sunglasses to protect himself if he had to fire it. "It could just be a couple of privates who didn't get the memo. Or they might be kind-hearted locals who think I'm just a harmless recreational wingsuiter, and they simply want to offer me a ride into town."

"It could also be a Humvee full of Guardians who spotted you on your descent," Doc cautioned him. "So pay attention to the insides of their left wrists. We're climbing into our vehicles at the airbase now," Doc told him. "We'll be there asap. Stay cool and don't hurt anyone—or let them try to hurt you—until we get there."

"Roger that," Rafe said calmly. "Pay attention to the speed limit."

"Don't you worry about us," Doc told him. "We'll be there soon!"

"Keep your radios open," the voice from the Situation Room told them. "Colonel, if you have a problem, try to pull your chute down. We'll see that."

"Understood," Rafe replied.

The vehicle pulled up moments later with four suspicious-looking occupants. Rafe was on high alert before it came to a stop. Though the four men in the vehicle wore Army fatigues, they didn't have military haircuts. Even odder, they all wore long sleeve shirts despite the hot afternoon sun. So Rafe couldn't check for tattoos.

"Pretty impressive flying," the driver said to Rafe while looking him over closely.

"Thanks!" Rafe shot back. "Did you drive all the way out here to tell me that?"

"No, actually, we're camping out here," the driver replied unconvincingly.

"That's odd," Rafe replied. "I was under the impression that this area is closed to traffic. And I didn't see a campsite as I circled overhead for the nearly 20 minutes."

"I guess you missed it then," the driver said with an edge in his voice. "And no one's said anything to us about the area being closed. If it is, how did you plan on getting out of here?"

"I'm actually with the Army Corps of Engineers, surveying and testing rock stability in the region," Rafe explained. "I just jump for fun."

"Fun, huh?" the driver replied. "Where'd you jump from?

"A plane," Rafe said simply.

"Must have been awfully high," the driver remarked. "We didn't see or hear one."

"Well then, you must not have been paying close enough attention," Rafe shot back.

"Oh, we've been paying attention," the driver said ominously. "Haven't we men?"

"Sure have!" a back-seat passenger said and pointed a 9mm semi-automatic pistol at Rafe.

"Whoa, fellas!" Rafe shouted. "Did I break a law or something?"

"We're the ones who break the law," the driver shouted back. "Put your hands up!"

"Who are you? What have I done?" Rafe shouted, hoping his radio was picking everything up and that those listening already knew whether or not the men were Guardians.

"One of you guys in the back seat hop out and make room for our birdman, here," the driver ordered. "And birdman—get out of that ridiculous suit and hop in."

Rafe figured that was his one and only chance to get the drop on the four goons. So he bent at the waist, grabbed a zipper at the bottom of one leg of the suit, and quickly pulled it up. When his hand reached his waist, Rafe pulled his stun weapon from his belt, squeezed and held the trigger and knocked the four desperadoes out before they knew what hit them.

"Did any of you hear all this?" Rafe shouted in the direction of his helmet.

"Loud and clear," the voice from the Situation Room replied.

"Roger that!" Doc shouted back as he raced north on Interstate 17 toward Sedona.

"What was that strange noise?" the voice from the Situation Room asked.

"It's classified," Rafe answered simply. "And very effective."

"Nice work, Rafe!" Doc said over the radio. "How long will they be unconscious?"

"Roughly 20 minutes," the colonel answered.

"Hop in the driver's seat and haul all four of them up out of sight in the shadows of the mountains," Doc told him. "Chastain may already know you're there, but take your chute with you just in case he doesn't. No sense making it easy for him."

"The chute 's bundled, and all the hombres are aboard Doc," Rafe said as he hit the driver's seat with his helmet in his lap and drove the Humvee deep into a nearby gorge.

Rafe set the parking brake on the Humvee and off-loaded his four-man cargo. He lifted each of them with a fireman's carry and lined them up shoulder-to-shoulder in the shade against a boulder and bound their wrists behind them with zip-ties he found in the Humvee. As Doc had guessed, each bore the "Guardian" tattoo on the inside of his left wrist.

"You were right, Doc," Rafe said into the microphone in his helmet. "They're Guardians. Do you want me to ask them anything in particular when they wake up, or do you just want me to babysit them until you get here?"

"Just sit tight with them," Doc said. "And keep them quiet in case any others come looking for them. We'll be there in less than an hour. Smoke 'em if you got 'em, Colonel."

"If you insist," Rafe answered

The Legionnaire sat on the hood of the Humvee with his weapon in his lap, his helmet beside him. He took his sunglasses off, rubbed his eyes, and took a swig from his canteen. He knew it might be the only quiet moment he'd have for a while. So he rested against the vehicle's windshield, lit a cigar from the leather humidor he kept in the thigh pocket of his uniform, and drew the satisfying smoke into his tired lungs while he waited for the Guardians to awaken.

## 10

## "THIS MUST BE HELL"

**R**oughly 15 minutes later, the two Guardians on the left awoke and shook their heads.

"Welcome back!" Rafe said to them. "How'd you sleep?"

"Fuck you!" the one on the end shouted back. "You're a dead man!"

"Well, then this must be hell, 'cause it sure ain't heaven," Rafe replied snidely.

"You don't know what hell is yet!" the Guardian shouted. "But you will very soon!"

"Actually, I'm looking for your hideout," Rafe said. "Care to show me where it is?"

"I'll be happy to take you there," the other Guardian said, "and when we get there, you'll wish you'd never met us!"

"If you're going to be that way about it, go back to sleep," Rafe said and fired another round at the two of them. He noted the time for his feedback on the stun gun's performance. Moments later, the same scenario unfolded when the other two Guardians awakened.

"Everything okay, Colonel?" the voice from the Situation Room asked over the radio.

"What is it you Americans say?" Rafe asked with a chuckle. "Everything's just peachy?"

"That's good to hear," the voice answered. "How do you say that in French?"

"Tout va comme sur des roulettes," Rafe said with a thick French accent.

"Sounds sexy," the voice said, "but it just doesn't have the same ring to it."

"What's that mean?" Rafe asked defensively.

"It's difficult to explain," the voice said. "Just stick with the American version."

All four Guardians were still unconscious when Doc's voice came on the radio again.

"Rafe, come in," he said. "We're headed up from the trailhead."

"Hello, Doc! You're missing a great slumber party!" Rafe replied and fired off a flare he'd found stowed in the Humvee with the zip-ties.

*So much for not attracting attention,* Doc said in his head and stirred his truck off the trail and into the deep gorge he'd seen the flare ascend from.

"Well, I see why you called it a slumber party," Q said when he arrived and saw the Guardians unconscious and slumped against one another.

"How long have they been out?" Doc asked. "Do they have a radio with them?"

"Six minutes exactly for the two on the left," Rafe replied and jotted the time on his note pad. "Five minutes, seven seconds for the other two. I didn't find a radio. I don't imagine it would pick up a signal from inside the mountain."

Doc walked over to the Guardians and raised the left arm of one of them. When he saw the distinct "Guardian" tattoo and let go, the arm fell to the ground with a thud.

"They're out, alright," he told Rafe. "Your gun appears to be as effective as our PHASR rifles. When they awaken, will they remember being stunned?"

"Not for a while," Rafe replied. "Some never do. But they all awaken with a headache."

"The memory loss is consistent with the PHASR's after-effects," Doc said. "We were never around when our targets awoke. But I've heard about the headaches. So I assume they awoke in a bad mood."

"Affirmative," Rafe replied, "which makes it difficult to persuade them to cooperate. But I've never fired a second round before. So I'm interested to find out if a second dose puts them in a different mood."

"Let's hope it makes them cooperative," Doc said. "Hopefully, they can get us in."

"What'll we do with them if they're not cooperative?" Q asked.

"We'll cross that bridge when we come to it," Doc replied.

"Let's find out right now," Rafe said.

"How exactly do you propose we do that?" Doc asked incredulously.

Doc watched in amazement as Rafe held a small device the size of a penlight close to an ear of a Guardian, who awoke instantly.

"Welcome back!" Rafe told the Guardian cheerfully. "How'd you sleep?"

"Pretty good, actually," the Guardian said. "Who are all of you, and what am I doing here?"

"Are you really that stupid or just pretending?" Q asked sarcastically.

"I think it's best if I handle the questioning, Q," Doc interrupted, amazed at Rafe's ability to awaken a target so easily. "Do you know where we are? What's the last thing you recall?"

"I was riding in the back of the Humvee on routine patrol of the area," the Guardian said.

"What area?" Doc asked again.

"We were in the mountains north of Sedona, " the Guardian answered. "Why am I tied up? Are you police?"

"We're friends of the Keeper, and we're trying to find him," Doc said and hoped for the best. "We just happened to find you guys. If we untie you, can you take us to him?"

"Sure," the Guardian said happily. "Cut me and my partners loose, and I'll gladly take you to the Keeper."

"Cut 'em loose, Q," Doc ordered and disregarded Q's look of total skepticism.

Doc and company were all pleasantly surprised just minutes later when all four Guardians were happily back in their Humvee and leading the way to Baird's hideout.

"How can you trust them, Doc?" Jenny asked as Doc drove close behind the Guardians.

Q asked the same question over the radio from the trailing vehicle.

"Washington, are you there?" Doc asked the voice in the Situation Room.

"We are, Doc," the voice answered. "What are you thinking?"

"I'm thinking this is our best option," Doc replied. "We're flying by the seat of our pants here, and my gut tells me our chances are better *with them* than *without them*."

"Agreed," the voice said flatly. "Rafe, where did you see the entrance to their hideout?"

"It's under a sandstone outcropping in the side of the mountain we're headed to," Rafe answered. "Gabriel didn't have enough time to create it. So it must be a natural cavern he discovered. Baird's Guardians probably worked on it while he and Gabriel were gone. There's no telling what we'll find once we're inside. What's worse, they might know we're about to arrive, thanks to Gabriel."

"Maybe…and maybe not!" Madeleine reminded Doc.

"I vote for 'maybe not,'" Noah chimed in.

"To complicate things further, we'll lose contact once you're inside," the voice added.

"Roger that!" Doc said resolutely. "Q, stick close behind me. Hit the gas as soon as the door opens. Whether they're expecting us or not, you know they'll see us when the door opens, so drive right past the Humvee and keep going as far as you can. If anyone gets in your way, run 'em over."

"Now you're talking like the Doc I know!" Q said. "Have your weapons ready and hang on everybody! We're about to do what we do best!"

"Do what you must!" Rafe stood up and shouted. "But remember, Gabriel is mine!"

"May we all do the best we ever have!" Louis said from the passenger seat.

"Roger that!" Jenny replied from the seat behind him. "I love you, Louis!" she said softly.

"Be careful, my darling!" Louis replied over his shoulder and reached out for her hand. "I love you too!"

"And I love you both!" Q said in his familiar, flippant way.

When the Guardians reached the outcropping they honked the Humvee's loud air horn three times, and a large sandstone slab slowly swung inward to reveal a huge, well-lighted cavern. As planned, Doc and Q stomped on their gas pedals and raced past the Humvee, into the unknown. As the vehicles rolled to a stop, the team bailed out with their weapons at the ready and took cover, expecting a hail of bullets. But the bullets didn't come. Instead, a crowd of Guardians quietly gathered between the team and the way they came in.

"Stay alert," Doc quietly ordered his team. "But don't

shoot unless we're fired upon."

"I hate that rule," Q whispered.

"Roger that!" Louis whispered back under the vehicle.

"We're looking for the Keeper and Nostradamus!" Doc said loudly. "Are they here?"

"Who are you, and why do you seek them?" a Guardian asked.

"We friends and we need to speak to them about a plan for the future," Rafe said.

"They are not available," the Guardian said. "You will have to come back."

"I'm afraid we cannot leave without speaking with them," Doc said forcefully. "The future can't wait, and neither can our discussion about it."

"Nostradamus knows the future, and he and the Keeper are busy planning for it," the Guardian replied tersely. "And I can assure you that they have things under control."

"Well, you see, that's exactly what we need to speak with them about," Doc replied. "They are unaware of some critical facts about the very near future. We're here to make those facts clear to them, and we must insist on doing that face-to-face."

Doc's tone told Q something would have to give quickly in order to avoid force. He rested his left hand on his brand new holstered 9mm Browning Hi-Power Mark III and silently raised his hand shoulder-high as a signal to the team to be ready to act at any moment.

"Well, I'm afraid you are asking the impossible," the Guardian said. "To begin with, you haven't even identi-fied yourselves. What would make you think you can simply show up here and meet with such powerful men who are engaged in such important planning?"

"Please forgive our rudeness," Rafe quickly replied in a last-ditch effort to avoid using deadly force that could prevent him from saving his friend. "I'm Lieutenant Colonel Alexandre Rafael Bellarose of France's 2nd Foreign Legion Parachute Regimen. And these are my team members and friends, who have accompanied me to ensure the success of my efforts to meet with Nostradamus. You see, the future of France and the rest of the world is important to us also. And as my friend explained, we are in possession of important informa-tion we can only share with them face-to-face. So I implore you to allow us to do that without further delay."

*What a load of horse dung!* Q thought to himself. "Let's blast them already, grab Baird and the spooky Frenchmen and get out of here! Come on, Doc! I count 47 of 'em. They're six deep. I know you can see that most of them are armed. But the ones in back can't do a thing bunched up the way they are. Stop trying to avoid the inevitable. Do it now, before they spread-out and gain the advantage! Do it! Now!"

Still, the disciplined team of seven silently faced-off against overwhelming odds. Louis, Jenny, Madeline, and Noah slowly unsnapped their sidearms and watched Q's raised right hand out of the corners of their eyes. They knew the U.S. Marshal had an uncanny sense of when Doc wanted them to spring into action. It was all they had to go on in that heart-stopping moment.

Doc had watched closely and instinctively knew Rafe had failed in his final attempt to avoid violence. He also knew the Legionnaire's primary objective was to retrieve his compatriot.

"Find Chastain!" Doc yelled at the Legionnaire, then drew his 16-round EDC X9 pistol. Q instantly dropped his right hand, and the team members all drew their weapons.

"Eeeeasy," Doc said calmly and exhaled as his team filled-in around him and took aim at the front row of Guardians. "Don't anyone move!" he told the Guardians forcefully. "My friend's just going to look around. No need to do anything we'll all regret."

Doc and Q both knew the look they saw in the Guardians' eyes.

"Spread out slowly," Q quietly said to the rest of the team. "Get ready to take cover and don't fire unless we do."

Jenny, Noah, Madeline, and Louis all locked like lasers on the Guardians and slowly stepped back in the direction of the vehicles they'd rode in on. Rafe found a corridor and headed down it.

"Stop them!" a Guardian at the front of the crowd shouted and fired a Glock G45 at Doc.

Q put a .40 caliber hollow point bullet between the Guardian's eyes with such speed and accuracy. It surprised even Doc. The cavern instantly filled with the deafening blasts, echos, and reverberations of gunfire, smoke, and the powerful smell of gunpowder.

When the noise stopped and the smoke cleared, 33 Guardians lay dead. The remaining 14 dropped their weapons and surrendered. Q had a wound in his left thigh, and a bullet had creased Jenny's head, just above her right temple. As she lay bleeding on the ground, Louis crouched over her and refused to lower his weapon until Doc and Noah had put zip-ties on every prisoner's wrists and ankles. Madeleine tore the hem of her blouse away and wrapped it around Jenny's wound.

"Who's hit?" Doc turned and asked in the hope no team member had been.

"Jenny and Q," Louis answered. "Jenny's just creased. She'll be okay."

"I'll be fine too," Doc grunted as he leaned against a vehicle and used his belt as a tourniquet on his leg.

He grumbled at Madeleine when she tried to help him, but ultimately let her clean his wound with water from a canteen and dress it in gauze she got from a first-aid kit in the truck Q was leaning against.

"Jenny, you stay here and make sure Q doesn't shoot any more Guardians unless he absolutely has to," Doc said. "The rest of you follow me. Keep your eyes peeled for anywhere Chastain could have stashed the missing scrolls and the flash drive, and hope we find Rafe before he finds more trouble."

"Be careful, you guys," Q called out to them as they headed toward the corridor Rafe had taken. "And come back soon. I don't know how I can resist giving one of these Guardians a wound just like mine!"

"Rafe!" Doc shouted down the corridor. "Rafe, can you hear me?"

Doc desperately wanted to bring the assault to a conclusion while his team had still not sustained any lasting damage. He hoped they wouldn't encounter more than a very few more Guardians before locating Rafe, and that they'd be able to quickly subdue and extract Chastain and Baird and be on their way back to Luke Air Force Base for the return to D.C.

"Rafe, can you hear me?" Doc shouted again, about 50 yards down the corridor.

"I'm here, Doc!" Rafe's voice echoed off the stone walls. "I got 'em both! Turn right about 100 yards in, and you'll see me! Come help me get them out of here!"

At the turn, Doc could see several Guardians unconscious in a heap. About 100 feet beyond the heap, he could see Rafe kneeling between two prone bodies Doc assumed were Chastain and Baird.

*Thank God, it's over!* the former SEAL thought. His next thought was, *Lord, please let us get out of here quickly and with no other casualties.*

Rafe quickly rifled through Chastain's and Baird's pockets, in the one-in-a-million chance that one or the other had the flash drive on him. But neither had it.

"No luck here," Rafe told Doc. "But I found them in the only office, just inside that door. I believe it's the only office in here."

"Noah, run back and bring a truck here so we can take these two with us!" Doc shouted excitedly. "Everyone else, tear into that office and find the flash drive, and then let's get out of here!"

Doc pulled a half-dozen zip-ties from a pocket in his cargo pants and handed three to Rafe.

"Tie Chastain up any way you see fit," Doc told him. "I'll do the same with Baird, and we'll be out of here in no time."

"Roger that!" Rafe said as he took the zip-ties from Doc.

As the zip-tying was completed, Noah came around the corner in the truck, and Doc hurriedly joined his team in the office to help with the hunt for the scrolls and flash drive.

"They'll be unconscious at least another ten minutes," Rafe told Noah. "I can load them onto the truck on my own. You should probably help your team find the missing materials so we can get out of here."

Eleven and a half minutes later, Baird slowly awoke and looked at Rafe through two swollen, bloodshot eyes.

"Welcome back," the Legionnaire said. "Sorry for the zip-ties. They're purely procedural, and we'll take them off the moment we can. Did you sleep well? How do you feel?"

"My head hurts," Baird mumbled. "Who the hell are you, and what have you done?"

"I'm a friend of your friend over there," Rafe said, with a nod toward Chastain, who was still unconscious.

"What do you want?" Baird asked in anger.

"I'm here to take my friend home where he belongs," Rafe answered.

"You can never pull that off alone," Baird told him.

"Oh, I'm not alone," Rafe told him. "Here come my friends now."

Baird looked in the direction Rafe was pointing and saw Doc and his team emerge from the office and walk toward the truck.

"Captain John Henry Holiday!" Baird said sardonically.

"It looks like I just may be able to settle the score with you after all, my friend!"

"I'm not you're friend," Doc said through gritted teeth. "And the only score that's going to be settled today is you're being shipped back to Gitmo."

"I'll never return to Gitmo," Baird said with a laugh.

"I wouldn't be too sure of that," Doc replied.

"Oh, I'm sure alright," Baird assured him. "Nostradamus here told me so."

"Where are his scrolls, Baird?" Doc asked angrily, having failed to find them in the office.

"You'll have to ask him," Baird replied. "He is still alive, isn't he?"

"He is, isn't he?" Doc asked Rafe.

"Of course," Rafe said nervously. "But he should be awake by now."

Rafe pulled the pen-knife-size contraption from his shirt pocket and used it on Chastain. But the Legionnaire-gone-bad remained unconscious.

"This has never happened before," Rafe told Doc.

"We're leaving," Doc replied. "You've got your Legionnaire. The Situation Room's arranged for Homeland Security to escort us back to the airbase and mop up after us here. Let's move out!" Doc shouted, and led the team back to the trucks.

## 11

---

## THE HERO APPEARS

A s Doc's warriors readied to board the trucks and leave, he told Madeleine to drive the lead truck with Noah, her brother, and Chastain in the back.

"Jenny, Louis, and Q will ride with me and keep an eye on Baird in the bed of the second truck," Doc announced. "It's him the Guardians will want," he shouted to Q. "So tie him up nice and tight, up high in a chair where they'll be able to see him.

"We need to make it back out in the direction of the trailhead where we're supposed to rendezvous with a chopper the president promised us he'd have in the air and waiting for our signal. Madeleine, I want you to exit this cavern at max speed and don't slow down until you see a chopper approaching.

"You can bet more Guardians are patrolling the perimeter and will try to stop us when they see we have

Baird," Doc reasoned. "They may be willing to let us have Chastain, but they're going to do everything possible to keep us from hauling Baird back to prison. You can bet that if we're attacked, my truck will be their target. Your orders are to get Chastain aboard the chopper no matter what. It's mission-critical that you get him back to Luke Air Force Base asap, so they can load him onto a plane to France.

"If Guardians strike, we'll keep them too busy to bother with you. But no matter what happens, I want you to keep going as fast as this crate will carry you and don't look back. Understood?"

"That's not S.O.P., Doc!" Madeleine pushed back. "You won't cut and run if our truck gets waylaid. You can't order us to keep rolling without you!"

"That's *exactly* what I'm ordering you to do," Doc shot back firmly. "The president's already had far too much to apologize to the French for. We're not going to give him any more reasons if we can help it. The French are important allies. Our primary mission is to keep it that way. Baird will meet his end one way or another. But Chastain has a date with destiny, and we're going to do everything possible to make sure he keeps it. Is that clear?!"

"Clear as crystal!" Madeleine replied firmly, then climbed into the driver's seat of the lead truck and started its huge diesel engine. "Everyone aboard and ready to roll?" she leaned out the window and shouted to Noah and Rafe in the bed of the truck.

"Roger that!" Noah shouted back to her with a confident smile. "Let's do it!"

Doc took the wheel of the second truck and cranked the engine to a loud roar. He could see Q tying the last couple of knots in the rope that secured Baird and his chair in the truck's bed, tight up against its rear window.

"You lead a blessed life, Baird!" Q growled at the mad man and knotted the rope as tightly as he could. "If it were up to me, I'd just tie you into the chair and let it roll around in the bed while I took every curve and bump in the road at 90 miles an hour!

"I guess you somehow still have a place in Doc's heart," Q continued growling. "But he put me in charge of you, and I don't have a heart. So you'd better hope you don't need someone to save your neck on this ride because I don't consider your neck worth savin'!"

"You'll do whatever Doc tells you to do," Baird replied with a cocky smile. "You always do. That's why you are both still alive."

"You should have such a friend!" Q growled at him, then grabbed a dirty rag from the bed of the truck and stuffed it into Baird's mouth. "You've said all I want to listen to, you crazy son of a bitch. Chew on this until we get you aboard a plane back to Gitmo."

"Radio check," Doc said into his radio as he put his truck in gear.

"Back at you!" Madeleine responded.

"Put your emergency alert lights on and let's roll!" he told her.

"Roger that!" Madeleine said as she put her truck in gear and popped the clutch.

Back in the daylight, forty miles per hour seemed like 80 as the trucks rumbled down the rugged trail through the high desert.

"This is Doc. Come in!" the former SEAL barked into the radio.

"Welcome back, Doc!" the voice from the Situation Room replied. "Do you have the packages we're expecting?"

"Roger that!" Doc replied. "Do you have a chopper for us?"

"Twelve o'clock high and closing," the voice replied calmly. "All hands are to climb aboard once it sets down. Crewmen on board will drive your trucks back to the base."

"Oh my God!" Doc said as he leaned forward over the steering wheel and spotted a giant, desert drab Sikorsky CH-53K King Stallion helicopter about 1,000 feet in the air and descending fast. "Tell President Prescott thank you on behalf of our entire team!"

"Will do, Captain," the voice replied.

"Oh mon Dieu!" Rafe suddenly heard Chastain shout over the roar of the truck and the rushing wind. "It's a King Stallion! Rafe! Where are we?"

"Gabriel!" Rafe shouted back. "Is it really you? Are you back?"

"Back?" Chastain sat up in the truck bed and shouted. "Back from where?"

"I can't believe it!" Rafe said and hugged his friend tightly. "You're back! It's a miracle!"

"What'd I miss?" Gabriel asked innocently as he and Rafe and Noah bounced wildly in the bed of the racing truck.

"You have no idea!" Rafe shouted with a smile.

The chopper slowed about 200 feet above the ground and kicked up a dust cloud that engulfed the speeding trucks as it prepared to land.

"Hold it!" Doc shouted to Madeleine over the radio. "Give that monster room to land!"

"I can't believe my eyes, Rafe!" Chastain shouted. "I haven't seen one of those amazing birds since I test flew one nearly four years ago at Luxeuil Air Base! What a beauty she is!"

"What else do you remember?" Rafe asked Chastain excitedly.

But the Legionnaires didn't have time to answer. Gunfire

suddenly peppered the truck from all directions. Rafe, Chastain, and Noah flattened in the truck bed until the shooting stopped long enough for them to slip over the side and run toward the landing chopper along with Madeleine, Jenny, and Louis. Doc climbed into the bed of his truck and helped Q cut Baird loose from the chair.

"Why isn't that bird returning fire?" Q shouted.

"You're all going to die!" Baird shouted at Doc before Q knocked the madman out with the grip of his pistol.

Doc jumped to the ground, and Q helped get Baird into a fireman's carry on Doc's shoulder. Then the two of them raced behind the rest of the team into the chopper. The gunfire then rained on the chopper, and the team heard the cockpit glass shattering. By the time Doc, Q, Louis, and Rafe got to the flight crew, the pilot and co-pilot were gravely wounded, and the flight engineer was dead.

"Rafe!" Doc yelled. "Please tell me you can fly this thing!"

"Sorry, Doc! No can do!" Rafe answered with regret.

"I can!" Chastain shouted and sprinted into the cockpit, where Rafe and Louis were returning fire through windows whose glass had been shot out.

While Doc pulled the badly wounded pilot and co-pilot out of their seats and the line of fire, Chastain donned the pilot's helmet and took his place behind the controls.

The French hero of the first order pushed the throttle forward and took command of the foot pedals as the chopper again generated a massive dust cloud and slowly rose off the desert floor.

"Can you fire any of the weapons?" Doc shouted hopefully.

"Negative!" Chastain shouted back. "No ammo!"

"Get us the hell out of here!" Doc shouted over his shoulder as he and Q desperately administered CPR to the mortally wounded pilot and co-pilot just behind the cockpit.

A thick wall of sand prevented Louis and Rafe from seeing the Guardians they were shooting at through the shattered cockpit windows. Still, they returned fire until the Guardians finally ran out of ammunition. Jenny, Noah, and Madeleine did the same through windows that swung open in the aft section.

About fifty feet off the ground, Chastain gunned the choppers three 7,500 horsepower engines, and the massive airship shot skyward and forward at nearly 200 miles per hour.

"Incroyablei!" Chastain shouted excitedly over the sound of the wind rushing through the bullet-riddled cockpit. "Anyone care to fill me in regarding who was shooting at us?"

"It's…it's a short flight and very long story," Rafe said.

"I assume this bird is locked in on its home," Chastain told Rafe with a smile.

"It is," Doc interjected. "And it'll just about land itself when we get there."

"They've come a long way in the past four years," Chastain remarked.

"Haven't we all?" Q said wryly and raised an eyebrow at Doc.

"How do you feel, Gabriel?" Rafe asked his closest friend.

"Rested and ready for action!" Chastain answered. "How long did I sleep?"

"You won't believe the answer," Q assured him. "And I'll bet it's classified."

Three miles into the flight, the team began to breathe easier. That's when the stinger missile hit the tail rotor.

"Mayday! Mayday! We're going down!" Chastain yelled as he began to lose control of the chopper. "I'll do my best to put it down softly! But brace yourselves!"

"Is there any weapon those savages don't have?" Q shouted in frustration and anger.

"Easy team!" Doc shouted. "Be ready for a firefight when we hit the ground! Ready your weapons and ammo!"

Rafe discovered eight M16 rifles and dozens of ammo clips in a weapons chest at the rear of the cabin.

"Heads up!" he shouted to the team and tossed them each a rifle and clips.

"Set 'em on 'Full Auto'!" Doc shouted. "And somebody sit on Baird so he doesn't try anything!"

"I'm already kneeling on his back, Doc!" Q shouted happily.

"Heavy vehicles approaching!" Chastain yelled from the cockpit as the chopper began to spin out of control, and the Legionnaire struggled to slow its descent.

"Follow me!" Rafe told Noah as he ran to the cockpit to provide cover for Chastain.

Bullets again ripped through the fuselage while the chopper was still in the air, and the team returned fire with a vengeance. A half-dozen Guardians rushed the chopper the minute it hit the ground and scrambled to access the heavily damaged cockpit. Noah and Rafe quickly emptied their clips but had no time to reload before they were both fighting for their lives hand-to-hand. As four Guardians fiercely began to overpower Rafe and Noah, Chastain's training with the King Stallion years earlier caused him to instinctively reach under the pilot seat where he'd once before found a loaded M18 SIG Saure Modular Pistol strapped and ready.

He yanked the 9mm semi-automatic from its holster, disengaged the safety with a flick of his thumb as though he'd done it a thousand times, and instantly killed two Guardians as they tried to climb into the cockpit through the shattered windows. That left just the four still wrestling with Rafe and Noah.

"Help Rafe!" Noah shouted as he lifted the Guardian he had ahold of, body-slammed him out of the cockpit and followed after him back into the chopper's cabin with his SOG Bowie knife.

The other three Guardians had Rafe pinned in the co-pilot chair and were piled on top of him. Chastain smashed the grip of the SIG Sauer into the base of the nearest Guardian's skull, which knocked him out and sent him tumbling to the floor. Chastain could then see the other two were almost piggyback, trying with their combined strength and weight to drive a bayonet into Rafe's chest.

"Ahhhhhhh!" Rafe screamed as the tip of the blade sliced a half-inch into his sternum.

Chastain instantly pressed the barrel of the SIG Sauer to the temple of the Guardian holding the knife and pulled the trigger. Less than an eye-blink later, he did the same to the Guardian on top. Both dead men slid to the floor, but the blade was still stuck in Rafe's chest. Chastain reflexively pulled it out and thrust into the neck of another Guardian who was climbing into the cockpit.

"Merci!" Rafe said breathlessly and held his chest wound.

"Vous êtes les bienvenus!" he (You're welcome!) replied and helped Rafe to his feet.

The Legionnaire-turned-pilot then ran halfway through the cabin, slid the rest of the way across the floor to the weapons locker, snatched the last two M16 rifles, inserted clips and threw one to Rafe. By then, every member of the team silently wondered if any of them would make it out of the ravaged chopper alive. No matter how many Guardians they shot, more rushed into the chopper right behind them. And there was still no sign of help arriving from the airbase.

"Rafe, zap Baird with that ray gun of yours!" Q yelled to the Legionnaire across the cabin.

The marshal needed to be able to move about freely, which he couldn't do while struggling to control Baird. Plus, Q figured Baird being unconscious would make it much more difficult for the Guardians to exit the chopper with him. Doc heard Q's plea and understood his friend's logic, but thought better of it.

"Let him up, Q!" Doc shouted. "But don't zap him, Rafe!"

"What are you thinking, Doc?" Q shouted back as he got off of his captive's back.

Baird instantly sprang to his feet and started moving toward the cabin door, which his Guardians had all but blown off its hinges and were still entering through.

"Hold your fire!" Doc yelled. "Put your weapons down!"

It was a calculated risk the former SEAL captain felt he must take. The seasoned commander within him knew he was about to lose Baird, whether his entire team died or somehow lived through the vicious assault. He had decided to let Baird go in the hope that it satisfied the Guardians and they'd stop fighting and cut and run with him. His gamble paid off because Baird was anxious to end the shooting too.

"Let's move out *NOW*, before we have to fight the whole army!" the madman ordered his Guardians.

What Doc hadn't counted on was that Baird still wanted Chastain despite the Legionnaire having returned to sanity.

"Bring Nostradamus and let's go!" Baird shouted to the three Guardians who had Chastain surrounded.

The trio grabbed Chastain and started for the open door. But Rafe was determined to stop them.

"Look away and block your eyes!" Rafe yelled to the other members of the team as he drew his stun gun, blocked his own eyes, and blasted all four men.

As the men instantly blacked out and fell in a heap, more Guardians bolted into the chopper cabin to retrieve them. The first one to enter shot the stun gun out of Rafe's hand. The second one knocked him to the floor with the butt of an M16. Q reflexively moved to defend the bold Frenchman, but Doc grabbed his arm.

"We'll fight another day, I promise you," Doc quietly

told his friend as still more Guardians rushed in and dragged Chastain out of the chopper.

Doc and his team watched as Baird and his unholy army retreated into the desert with Chastain in tow.

"I hope we don't end up hating ourselves for this," Q sighed at Doc's side.

"We had Chastain and let him go," Rafe said firmly. "Success was literally within my grasp, and I've failed. *We've failed*! My country does not have its hero, and your president does not have the scrolls."

"We haven't failed, Rafe," Doc assured him. "We're alive, and so is Chastain. The only other possible outcome would have been a failure. This is merely the quiet between battles.

"I vow to each of you that though justice has been delayed, it will not be denied," Doc stated firmly. "We *will* end this madness. It's going to take longer than I'd hoped. But I promise you, we will bring this mission to a successful end! I don't know exactly how, and I don't know exactly when, but we *will* end it. And when we do, *we will end it once and for all!*"

What Doc couldn't bring himself to say out loud was that by the time Baird, Chastain, and the small army of Guardians had vanished—and long after a platoon from the airbase finally arrived—he *did* feel as though he had failed. The gnawing in his gut worsened when he overheard Madeleine quietly try to console Rafe, who felt he, too, had failed his fellow Legionnaire and dearest friend —and failed France.

"Doc always says everything happens for a reason," Madeleine softly told her brother. "In the time that I've known him, I've got to tell you, somehow, even the darkest times have worked out for the best. So I figure there's got to be something to it."

"Personally, I think it's a load of crap!" Rafe said in anger and frustration. "We had Gabriel. Now he's gone, and we have no idea where to find him! He's certainly not going back to Sedona! And we haven't got a clue where to look next! Are you honestly telling me you know this happened for a reason?"

"I cannot say that I know it, Alexandre," Madeleine tried to calm her brother a final time. "But I *can* say that it's what I will hold onto until I see otherwise," Madeleine said quietly, "So I hope you'll give it a try for the sake of your own spirit and peace."

"I'm afraid I'm not there yet, Sis," Rafe told her dejectedly. "I certainly can't use that line when we get to the base and I try to explain this to Ambassador LeCarre. If I had any less honor, I'd put Doc on the phone and make *him* explain how 'everything happens for a reason.'"

Rafe's words stung Doc painfully. Yet, the Frenchman's hunch that Chastain wouldn't return to Sedona opened Doc's mind to a sorely needed positive thought. He felt Rafe might be right. Chastain probably had the flash drive hidden on him when they found him. But in the heat of the battle, they failed to search him thoroughly. It also made sense that when Chastain resurfaced and fought alongside the team, he very likely had no memory of the flash drive or the information it contained. So for the brief time that Chastain fought alongside the team, the flash drive most likely had been within their reach. Doc silently wrestled with that realization on the ride back to the airbase. But the potential implications were too ominous for him to keep bottled up inside. So he huddled with Q in the hope of sorting it out.

"What's up?" Q asked, sensing the urgency in Doc's eyes.

"Q, I believe that when Chastain left Sedona as Nostradamus, he had the flash drive on him. But after Rafe zapped him and he awakened as himself, he had no memory of the drive. That would explain why it never came up while he was with us.

"Now the question is will he again think he Nostradamus when he awakens from the second blast Rafe gave him. But whomever Chastain believes he is, you can bet Baird will snatch the flash drive for his Forbidden Library the moment he discovers Chastain has it. And believe it or not, that would be our lucky break!"

"How so, Doc?" Q asked with doubt dripping from his lips.

"It means the flash drive is no longer hidden in some unknowable nook or cranny in the mountains of Sedona. So the odds seem stacked in our favor that we'll find the flash drive when we find Baird."

"That makes a lot of sense," Q agreed. "But it also means Baird either already has the drive, or he will have it very shortly."

"You're right," Doc replied. "We flushed Baird out of hiding like a scared rabbit. And knowing him, he'll be off to a new destination soon. He's proven he can elude the satellites. So we've done all we can here. It's time to regroup. So it's back to D.C. early tomorrow morning."

"I'm all for that!" Q replied and headed off to let the rest of the team know.

An hour later, Chastain regained consciousness as Nostradamus. He didn't remember fighting alongside Doc's team and Rafe, his best friend and brother-in-arms. But he very clearly remembered that the flash drive containing his prophesies was safely hidden in his left boot. He had no idea that two of the world's most powerful nations even knew it existed, and that they desperately wanted the scrolls it contained.

## 12

## DEFENDING HI-CATOCTIN

The sun was long gone on that dark, moonless Maryland night at Camp David, when Doc called Connie, as he did every night they were apart. He needed to hear her voice—and her laugh.

"Hello, Beauty," Doc said tenderly. "How are you? Have you been able to relax and enjoy Camp David?"

"Hello, John!" Connie replied excitedly. "I love you and miss you so! I'm fine here. They're treating us wonderfully. How are you? Are you safe and being careful?"

"I love you and miss you too, Beauty!" Doc answered. "We had a rough day today, but we're all safe. I just had to hear your voice and know *you're* okay."

"I'm more than okay, John," she answered. "Honey, I hear it in your voice. Something's wrong. What is is? Has someone been hurt?"

"No, I assure you everyone's safe and sound here, Connie," Doc assured her. "I'm sure Q will call Marsha shortly. But like I said, I needed to hear your voice. Beauty, I also need you to promise you'll be on your guard. The Secret Service is the best security force in the world. But today I saw Guardians fight more fiercely and in greater numbers than ever before.

"I pray they're all out here, too busy and spread too thin to pose a threat in D.C.," he told the love of his life. "But there's no way to be sure. Baird's money can wreak havoc anywhere in the world. No one is ever completely safe from the evil in his heart. So I will not rest as long as his dark heart is still beating. But I need to know you are being protected—and being careful."

"I am, John—and so is Marsha. I promise you that. But now I need you to promise me that you will finish this mission and come home to me as soon as possible. Do you promise?"

"I give you my word, Beauty!" Doc promised her sincerely. "And when I get back, you and I must talk about where we want to spend the rest of our lives together. Sound good?"

"That sounds wonderful, John darling," Connie said as her eyes teared up at the sound of the words she had feared she might never hear. "I'll be waiting eagerly for your return, darling!"

"I promise to be there the moment I can," Doc

answered. "In the meantime, be safe and sleep tight, my love!"

"I will, dear heart—and I pray you will also," she answered as they ended the call.

Connie hung up the secure phone and headed out of her room to find Marsha. But as she rounded a corner in one of several winding halls in the large cottage they'd moved into, she nearly collided with Christopher Donnalin, the young rookie Secret Service special agent who'd been assigned to ensure she and Marsha were comfortable during their stay at the compound.

"Whoa!" Donnalin chuckled as he braced Connie by her shoulders to steady her. "Excuse me, Mrs. Holiday. I didn't hear you coming."

"Oh, it's completely my fault," Connie said. "I'm just in a hurry to find my friend."

"Well, let's find her together," Donnalin suggested and offered her his arm.

Connie happily took hold of his elbow, gratified by the gesture and cheered by the thought that meeting this chivalrous young man might mean there were more in his generation. Their search for Marsha made Connie aware of how large and relatively empty the building was. But Connie grew increasingly uneasy as she contemplated the conversation she'd just had with Doc, and she became aware of how empty and remote the camp was when not in official use.

"Does the compound have an armory, Special Agent Donnalin?" Connie asked as casually as she could.

"Why, yes," Donnalin said, surprised by the question.

"Do you think I might be able to see it?" Connie pressed in her most innocent voice.

"I-I suppose so," Donnalin stuttered. "Do you have an interest in weapons?"

"Somewhat," she said simply. "I've been exposed to a great many since I met my husband. And he sometimes brings new ones home. So I'd love to be able to tell him about the weapons you have here."

"I suppose I could show you the primary armory where we keep our more common weapons," Donnalin said. "Of course, I'll have to clear it with my superior first. He's just down the hall. So it won't take long."

"Thank you so much," Connie said and settled onto a nearby settee.

Donnalin acted cool, but Connie's request to see the armory was the most off-the-wall he'd received in his short career. So he wasn't sure how his superior, Special Agent In Charge Austin Worthy, would respond to it when he knocked on his office door.

"Come in," Worthy barked in his routine voice.

"Excuse me, sir," Donnalin said tentatively, "but I've agreed to give Mrs. Holiday a brief tour of the building, and she's asked to see our armory."

"And?" Worthy prompted Donnalin for more info.

"Well sir, I just wasn't sure I should oblige her without checking with you first," Donnalin said.

"Special Agent Donnalin, did you read Mrs. Holiday's and Mrs. Marshall's files prior to their arrival?" Worthy asked calmly.

"I did, sir," Donnalin answered.

"So you know they both have 'Special Envoy to the President' status with 'Top Secret' security clearances, correct?" Worthy prompted the young agent.

"I do, sir," Donnalin answered.

"And do you also understand that Mrs. Holiday is the wife of retired Navy SEAL Captain and Secret Service Special Agent John Henry Holiday, who still serves the president in the highest classified capacity?" Worthy asked next.

"I do, sir," Donnalin repeated himself almost apologetically.

"And of course you also understand that Mrs. Marshall is the wife of U.S. Federal Marshal Quinton Marshall, who is also on special assignment to the president in an equally classified capacity, correct?" Worthy asked next.

"I do, sir," Donnalin again repeated himself.

"Special Agent Donnalin, is it really necessary for you to involve me in a decision regarding whether or not you should grant either Mrs. Holiday or Mrs. Marshall such a simple request?" Worthy finally asked.

"No sir! Not at all, sir!" Donnalin answered immediately.

"I'm extremely glad to hear that," Worthy answered encouragingly. "Keep up the great work, Special Agent Donnalin! Is there anything else you wish to discuss?"

"No sir!" Donnalin answered hurriedly. "I'd better get back to work now, sir."

"Carry on!" Worthy replied cheerfully.

Donnalin hurried back to Connie with a slightly flushed complexion.

"I apologize for the delay, Mrs. Holiday," he said politely. "If you will kindly follow me, I'll be happy to show you the armory."

"Thank you, Mr. Donnalin!" Connie said with her sweetest smile.

Along the way, Connie memorized the twists and turns, the long, curved stairway that took them to the elevator, and the button Donnalin pushed to reach the armory.

"Here we are," the special agent said as he opened heavy solid oak double doors to reveal a vault door with a touch screen embedded in the middle.

Donnalin pressed his palm to the screen, then opened the armory door wide. Connie was shocked at the sight of so many weapons she didn't recognize. But she did quickly recognize the half-dozen M16s, more than a dozen Beretta M9 pistols and three tiny SIG Sauer P238s. Doc had taught her how to use each of them proficiently, but she didn't share that fact with Donnalin —or anyone else.

"My goodness, you have an awful lot of weaponry!" she said, feigning surprise.

"Yes, ma'am," Donnalin said proudly. "We're ready for any threat at any moment!"

"I believe you are," Connie agreed.

Donnalin closed the vault by again pressing his palm to the screen.

"How do you do that if something's wrong with your hand?" Connie innocently asked

"I use these," Donnalin said as he pulled two keys on a lanyard out from under his shirt.

"Why two?" Connie asked with a raised eyebrow.

"Two agents are supposed to unlock the vault simultaneously," Donnalin casually said. "But in a pinch, it makes no sense to need two agents to open it."

"Makes sense," Connie replied, stifling her surprise at such a breach of protocol.

The two of them returned upstairs, where they found Marsha sitting in the study on an overstuffed armchair with her feet propped up on a massive ottoman. From that comfortable seat, Marsha had a terrific view out a wide bay window to the densely forested property that gives the compound its serene, remote quality.

"Oh my, don't you look comfy cozy?" Connie poked fun at her close friend.

"I must admit, under the circumstances, this view beats even your front porch at the lake house," Marsha said as she smiled for the first time since she and Connie arrived. "It makes me feel a million miles from danger. I wish Q and Doc and the rest of the team were here with us."

"I'm confident they will be before too very long," Connie said hopefully. "Tomorrow, I must lobby President Prescott for some time here with everyone once they return. But right now, I believe it's dinnertime. Did you complete your dinner menu selection this morning?"

"I most certainly did!" Marsha gushed. "I can hardly wait to taste the Veal Scallopini Piccata! It looked so yummy on the menu! What did you pick, Connie?"

"I chose the Chicken Salad Keto Lettuce Wraps," Connie told her. "They looked incredible on the menu too!"

"You are such a healthy eater!" Marsha sighed. "I really should have thought twice before befriending a nurse who's built like a marathon runner. I keep hoping that someday I'll be as inspired and motivated as I am happy when I'm eating out with you."

"Don't be so hard on yourself, Marsha," Connie chuckled. "Your veal dish is a healthy, responsible choice. Will you be joining us, Special Agent Donnalin?"

"Please, call me Chris," Donnalin said as he gently touched a shoulder of each of the wives. "I'm afraid I must attend to a few things while you enjoy dinner. But if you'd like, I'll gladly give you a tour of the grounds when you've finished. The compound illumination is quite impressive at night."

"That sounds lovely, Chris!" Marsha said. "What do you say, Connie?"

"I'm all in for a walk in the fresh air to end the day — especially since I plan to have dessert!" Connie laughed, and the two of them followed Donnalin to the dining room.

"I should be back in about 45 minutes. How does that sound?" he asked as he pulled out their chairs and unfolded their linen napkins for them.

"Perfect!" Marsha answered cheerfully as she admired the dashing Special Agent whom she guessed was born about the same time as Jason, the son she and Q lost at birth.

Donnalin reappeared just as the two good friends finished sharing a "Death By Chocolate" that Marsha said was "divine."

"Chris, thank heaven you're back," Marsha said with a laugh. "I was tempted to order another helping!"

"Time for that walk I promised you ladies," Donnalin said with a smile and led them out a pair of polished rosewood French doors to a walking path lined with black-eyed Susans.

The night air was calm and comfortable. The moonless sky made the lighting of the grounds all the more dramatic and welcoming. Soft, indirect light marked the walks and landscaping, while brighter, colored lights gave the low, rustic buildings a stately presence.

"It's so beautiful and peaceful." Connie sighed, 15 minutes into the tour. "You have a heavenly assignment here, Chris. You must feel very fortunate."

"I do," Chris told her. "And I'd be even more pleased to just give guided tours of the grounds. The history of Camp David is immensely interesting. The Algonquian Indians originally called this area Hi-Catoctin, meaning 'place of many deer.' When President Franklin D. Roosevelt spent time here, he renamed it 'Shangri-La.' President Dwight D. Eisenhower again renamed it 'Camp David' in honor of his father and grandson, which stuck. The history of this place is fascinating, for sure. But my main responsibility is to secure and protect the present."

Just then, rustling in a nearby tree caught Donnalin's attention.

"I think it may be time to return the two of you to your building," he said calmly as he strategically placed himself between the wives and the rustling tree.

As he turned his head to look over his shoulder, a bullet traversed his skull from his left temple to his right, and he fell at the feet of Marsha and Connie. Marsha screamed and desperately tried to help him. But he was dead when he hit the ground, and Marsha vomited violently when his blood covered her hands. While Marsha struggled to breathe, Connie bent over Donnalin, ripped open his shirt, and yanked the armory keys from around his neck.

"Follow me, quickly!" she told Marsha and pulled her by the hand back through the French doors, down the curved stairway, and into the elevator to the basement. As the elevator doors closed behind them, the gunfire behind the women grew louder, more intense, and closer.

"Where are we going?" Marsha asked, still coughing for lack of breath. "Is it safe?"

"It's the safest possible place!" Connie assured her as she opened the double oak doors to reveal the gun vault.

"What's this?" Marsha asked warily.

"It's the armory," Connie said as she inserted each of the keys from around Donnalin's neck into the two keyholes on opposite sides of the vault door.

She turned one, then moved to the other and turned it. But the vault door didn't unlock.

"Quick! Stand here and turn this key on 'three,'" Connie told her friend hurriedly.

"One, two, three!" Connie said, then heard a click and yanked the door open.

"Wow!" Marsha exclaimed when she saw the arsenal behind the door. "Do you know how to use any of these?" she asked her best friend hopefully.

"A few," Connie said as she pulled down an M16, a Beretta M9 and two clips for each, then grabbed two tiny SIG Sauer P238s.

Connie quickly checked to confirm the weapons were loaded, then she switched off the P238s' safeties and handed one to Marsha.

"What am I supposed to do with this?" Marsha asked, afraid of the answer.

"If someone comes at you, shoot him!" Connie said as she stuck the M9 in the waistband of her slacks and hefted the big M16 rifle to check its weight and balance.

"*I can't shoot anyone!*" Marsha exclaimed.

"Well, you better if someone grabs *me!*" Connie said. "Stay close," she told her friend as they shut the vault door and pulled the keys out together.

The pair ran back to the now-dark dining room, where

Worthy and three other agents were firing out shattered windows at gunmen hiding in trees and the heavy underbrush.

"What are you two doing here?!" Worthy shouted at them. "Where's Donnalin?"

"We're here to help because he can't!" Connie shouted back and crouched behind an overturned dining table with Marsha.

Connie rested the stock of the M16 on the table's edge and took aim out a window, then squeezed the trigger and shredded the leaves and branches of a tree until a body fell from it.

"Gotchya!" Connie uttered softly as she took aim at a second treetop.

Worthy's training told him to shut Connie down and get her and Marsha to safety. But Connie was quite obviously a capable shot had just significantly improved his team's odds. So he bit his tongue and kept firing.

"Are you okay?" Connie asked Marsha, who was crouched behind her.

"I'm okay, I guess," her friend replied quietly.

"Just remember what I told you to do if someone grabs me!" Connie told her, half in jest.

"Do you have agents on the grounds?" Connie shouted to Worthy.

"Three, I hope!" he answered doubtfully. "But I can't get any response on the radio."

"I hope they're alright!" Connie answered.

But they were hoping against hope. All three agents already lay dead on the grass just a few yards from the building.

"Keep the faith and keep your heads down," Worthy told Connie and Marsha as he jammed a fresh 20-round clip into his 9mm Mark III. "I've alerted headquarters in the capital and our rescue is on the way!"

Until that help arrived, the five souls in the bullet-riddled dining room were on their own with two dozen Guardians closing in on the building on all sides. Worthy was about to begin firing again when he heard the alarms sound for the front and side entrances. He could tell by the way Connie handled the M16 that she knew how to use it. So he pressed her into service.

"Mrs. Holiday, I need you to cover our backs!" he yelled across the dining room to her.

"The name's Connie!" she said as she turned her attention to the dining room entrance.

"Mine's Marsha!" Marsha yelled too as she stretched to reach another dining table and turned it on its side to shield Connie and herself from anyone entering the dining room.

"You both can shoot, right?" Worthy asked hopefully.

"You bet we can!" Marsha answered with a calmness that surprised Connie. "Hand me that bigger pistol you have," Marsha said so calmly she surprised herself.

Connie handed Marsha the Beretta M9 and the extra 15-shot clip.

"It's got a kick to it and the trigger is heavy, but I know Q's taken you the gun range and you can handle it," Connie said.

"I've got this," Marsha assured her as they both peered around the table that shielded them from the dining room entrance.

The first two Guardians through the doorway were obviously amateurs. They stuck their Glocks around the door jam and fired blindly, then scrambled into the dining room in opposite directions. Connie cut down the one who ran to the left. Marsha shot the one who ran to the right and both Guardians fell lifeless to the floor.

"Great shot!" Connie told her.

"Thanks!" Marsha answered. "I think my adrenaline's kicked in."

"I'd say you're right!" Connie replied with a smile and relief as she fired off another dozen rounds at the doorway to delay the main attack she knew was coming.

In moments, the attack *did* come. It began when Guardians threw three smoke grenades into the room. They detonated with bright flashes and sent shock waves through the room that disoriented the five desperate souls fighting for their lives there.

As Connie began to blackout, she saw a group of four Guardians rush through the doorway, and she fired off what was left in her M16 at them. The barrage of 45mm shells she unleashed took out two of the invaders, but the other two stood over her as she lay helpless.

"Finish her," one told the other, who raised his Russian-made AK-12 and pointed it between Connie's eyes.

The Guardian hesitated firing the round just an instant too long, and he died on his feet when his spine was severed by the heavy, newly honed Japanese Masahiro cleaver Liam, the camp chef, threw from the kitchen door. Like the dead Guardian lying beside him, the one who was still on his feet reacted too slowly, and Liam rushed from the kitchen using his prized 30-inch wok as a shield. The Guardian did manage to fire a couple of rounds, but Liam swung the wok by its one heavy handle and knocked him unconscious.

Worthy recovered just in time to witness the chef in action.

"Nice work, Liam!" he shouted

That's when they noticed the shooting had ceased. They both craned their necks to survey the grounds just beyond the eight shattered windows along the dining room's south wall.

"The cavalry has arrived!" Liam shouted at the site of

Secret Service agents U. S. Marshals handcuffing Guardians under the nearby apple and pear trees.

Worthy stood up and enthusiastically shook Liam's hand.

"I've never been so happy to see you out of the kitchen, Liam," he said with a smile. "You're obviously a man of *many* talents!"

"The Belgian army trained me for more than just cooking," the chef told Worthy with a grin and a wink.

"I hope your modest demeanor can withstand a presidential commendation," Worthy said.

"I'm sure I can bear it, sir," Liam said with a smile of his own.

"Call me Austin," Worthy told him. "That's what everyone who saves my life calls me."

The newly arrived agents entered the dining room along with emergency medical personnel who revived Connie and Marsha and put them aboard separate emergency medical units for the convoy back to the White House.

"Do I have to tell you boys how glad I am to see you?" Worthy asked them wryly.

"We know we have your undying gratitude," one of them replied. "Pun intended."

"So how many of you can stay to help clean this mess up?" Worthy asked in jest.

"A 'restore crew' should be here any minute." another agent said. "But we're out of here right now."

"Thanks for all you do, fellas," Worthy sighed as a farewell.

"Thanks for staying alive until we could get here!" he heard one of them reply as they left.

## 13

### THE GRAND MYSTERIES

"Where am I?" Connie managed to ask when she awoke strapped to a gurney. "Is Martha okay?!" she frantically asked next.

"She appears to be fine. You both do," the attendant told her. "Just shaken by the experience. She's following right behind us. You're both going to Walter Reed Hospital. Were you two using those weapons we found at your sides?"

"Yes," Connie replied. "Does that surprise you?"

"A little," the attendant admitted. "That scene looked to have been quite a firefight."

"I'm just glad it's over," Connie sighed, then stiffened and excitedly asked, "How's Special Agent Worthy?"

"If he was in the dining room with the two of you, he's fine, as are the others who were with you," the attendant said. "I guess they were lucky to have you two there!"

Connie tried to rest under the restraints on the stiff gurney as the vehicle wound its way out of the mountains on the way to Walter Reed, where she'd spent her entire nursing career—and where she and Doc met. But the more she tried to relax, the more restricted she felt beneath the straps that secured her. Her breath began to quicken, and she feared she might have a panic attack if she didn't get out from under the straps—and she knew that wouldn't be possible until they reached the hospital.

As her pulse rose, Connie's mobile phone rang.

"That's got to be my husband!" she said frantically. "Would you please answer it for me? It's in the left pocket of my slacks."

The attendant retrieved the phone, and Connie dictated the PIN code to him.

"Hello?" he said into the phone. "Yes, she's right here. Hold on a moment while I put you on 'Speaker.'"

"Hi, honey!" Connie said and began to tear up. "It's such a relief to hear your voice!"

"How are you, my darling?" he asked lovingly. "I hope you don't mind me calling you twice in one day. The president called and told me what happened and got me patched through to you as soon as he could. Are you and Marsha okay?'"

"They tell me we're both going to be fine, John, really," Connie said earnestly. "I'm sorry to worry you so. I can hear it in your voice."

"Oh, I'm not worried, Beauty," Doc lied. "I just called to hear your voice one more time before going to bed. Q and I will be back in D.C. by noon tomorrow, and I'm going to bring you the biggest bouquet of flowers anyone in Washington, D.C. has ever received."

"They're taking us to Walter Reed," she told him. "So you know I'll be in the best of hands. I've wanted to get back there for a couple years. But I never imagined doing it this way."

"Believe me, I would prefer that you get there a different way too!" Doc told her and could finally laugh. "It's wonderful to hear your voice, Beauty. I'm so very glad you're okay!"

"That I am, thanks to your lessons at the shooting range, darling," she said warmly.

"Well, it certainly looks like they paid off in a big way!" he replied. "I know you must rest, so I'll hang up and wait for you to call me tomorrow when you can."

"It a date, my love," Connie said cheerfully, and the attendant ended the call and put her phone in the ziplock bag that held her shoes and jewelry.

Doc's call transformed Connie's state of mind. She could finally rest and quickly fell asleep despite the bumps and shakes of the ride. She fell asleep knowing she'd soon be among old friends at Walter Reed. And best of all, she had a wonderful dream that she and Doc were walking the shore of Flathead Lake below the lake house arm-in-arm at sunset.

While Connie slept and Doc tried to, the tragic Legionnaire who again called himself Nostradamus sat on a cot in a tent high in the Black Mountains, near the Arizona/Nevada border. He untied his boots, dug into the left boot's upper and pulled out the thumb-size prize that Rafe, Doc and his team—and Baird—were committed to finding. With his feet free of his Legion-issued boots, Chastain stretched-out on the cot and watched the campfire through the tent flaps he'd left tied open in order to enjoy the nighttime mountain breeze.

He was perplexed about having no memory of what happened after being attacked earlier in the day by unknown forces and hit by a blast from a weapon he didn't recognize. His mind was blank until he was suddenly safe and sound, resting on a cot, warmed by a campfire in the dead of night. He had a long list of questions for "the Keeper." But he was also exhausted.

As sleep approached, Chastain held the flash drive up in the darkness of his tent and viewed the dance of the campfire through the translucent red plastic until he could no longer stay awake. Then he tucked the flash drive into his shirt pocket, buttoned it shut, and fell asleep.

But Doc still couldn't sleep. The more he tried to, the more his heart dwelled on Connie

and the more his mind pondered the countless things he

knew and didn't know about Chastain and his supposedly prophetic scrolls. Doc knew that French and American intelligence agencies had been aware for months that the AWOL Legionnaire wrote a series of predictions on scrolls. He also knew the agencies disagreed regarding the veracity of those predictions. According to President Prescott, French experts had examined Chastain's early scrolls and quickly dismissed most of what he had written as simply "bad dreams."

But those same experts were shocked and amazed by how inexplicably accurate a number of his latest predictions had proven to be, and they sounded the alarm when a DGSE informant reported that Chastain claimed to have predicted and archived details of a plot to assassinate the presidents of France and the U.S. during an upcoming summit conference.

The dilemma was that the two countries *were* planning a summit for the near future, and no credible, independent authority was able to confirm that Chastain had actually made such a prediction. The DGSE initially believed that *if* Chastain had, in fact, made such the prediction, it was among the scrolls he'd destroyed before being arrested. But when the informant disclosed that Chastain had archived all his predictions on a flash drive, the news triggered an international hunt for Chastain and the archive of his infamous scrolls.

The hunt for the scrolls had stalled efforts of the two nations to reach a vital bi-lateral agreement on their combined counter-terrorism efforts while the security forces of both nations scrambled to discover, understand and neutralize any threat to the success of the summit and the safety of Presidents DuPris and Prescott. When standard intelligence efforts failed to produce Chastain's scrolls, both nations committed the best special operations personnel they had to the hunt for what the classified record called "The Nostradamus scrolls." President Dupris called upon Rafe. President Prescott predictably assigned Doc and the team.

Doc took pride in the president's confidence in the team, but on this particular night, Doc was feeling the weight of this mission more than he'd ever felt on any other. Q felt it too and wandered from his bed out onto the patio at the rear of the barracks, where he found Doc sitting on a picnic table.

"You're still up, too," Q said to Doc, as though he'd guessed he would be.

"Who can sleep knowing what we know—and not knowing what we don't," Doc sighed.

"That's the truth, partner," Q agreed and sat shoulder-to-shoulder with his best friend.

The brothers-in-arms sat atop the table with their feet on the bench.

"They're going to be alright, right Doc?" Q asked about their wives with the first sound of fear Doc had ever heard from the tough U.S. Marshal.

"Guaranteed, Q!" Doc quickly reassured him. "Connie

would have told me if she thought otherwise—and she and I know enough of the staff at Walter Reed that someone would have called me if there was a reason to worry. You'll be hugging Marsha before noon tomorrow. I saw the president's personal 757 come in for a landing less than a half hour ago. By now, the ground crew's checking it out and getting ready to refuel it for our flight back to D.C. at 0600 hours. That much I'm sure of. It's everything else that's keeping me awake."

"Roger that," Q said quietly as he took off his trademark Stetson and fussed with it.

"I thought I might find you two out here," they heard Madeleine say behind them.

"Well hello, Bookworm!" Q said with feigned cheerfulness.

"*Bookworm?*" Madeleine shot back. "Where did that come from?" she asked indignantly.

"Now don't get all uptight about it, Madeleine," Q said. "It's a term of endearment."

"And that's the best you could come up with?" Madeleine asked in jest.

"Well, I guess it's because of Doc's story of first meeting you in a library," Q said.

"And in your mind, that makes me a 'bookworm'?" Madeleine pressed him further.

"You're in a very deep hole, Q," Doc chuckled. "I'd stop digging if I were you."

"Sorry, Madeleine," Q said. "I meant no offense."

"Oh, I know, Q," Madeleine said affectionately. "I was just teasing you in the hope of making you smile. Are Connie and Marsha still doing okay?"

"They are!" Doc answered. "And they'll be even better by morning."

"Got room for a few more out here?" Jenny asked cheerfully as she stepped out of the barracks, flanked by Louis and Noah.

"Well, the gang's all here," Q said to Doc. "Guess we're six sleepless peas in a pod."

"You all *really should* be getting some sleep," Doc told them.

"And you two don't need sleep?" Madeleine shot back.

"I don't know how much we *need it*, but I know we could both *use it*," Doc replied. "What we *need* is answers."

"Sometimes sleep brings them," Madeleine replied.

"I wish that were as true for me as they supposedly are for that Nostradamus character Chastain believes he is," Doc said to Madeleine as he began to pick her brain. "What's your best guess about him, Madeleine? Who are we really going up against? How do we capture him? What advantage does he give Baird?"

"Ah, those are some of the Grand Mystery of this mission," Madeleine said with a smile.

"The Grand Mysteries?" Doc repeated, hoping for an explanation he'd understand.

"The questions with no sure answers," she explained. "Each new 'Can Of Worms' that brought us our missions have had them."

"I guess I haven't been paying close enough attention," Doc said genuinely.

"Oh, you've paid close attention alright," Madeleine assured him. "But your focus is always on answers and solutions. Once a mission's accomplished, you move on to the next one and the new questions that come with it. If you dwelled on the questions that have no easy answers—or have no answers at all—we wouldn't have the successful track record you've led us to.

"Still, you mark my words, if and when the nation and the world ever learn of the places we've been, the extraordinary people we encountered and the near-impossible things we've accomplished, it will be the Grand Mysteries we encountered along the way that elevate our exploits from ordinary missions to legendary adventures."

"You've given this a lot of thought," Doc said with a raised eyebrow and a smile.

"An awful lot," Madeleine said to the friend she thought the world of. "I've written it all down too. Hopefully, the world will someday read all about it."

"That's a breach of security," Doc pointed out to her. "I hope you've secured it."

"You will never know where it's at unless and until I decide to share it with the world someday," Madeleine assured him.

"So you think it might make for interesting reading?" Doc asked with some surprise.

"Fantastic reading!" Madeleine gushed.

Madeleine now had Louis's and Jenny's rapt attention. They hoped she would finally provide some clues regarding what it was about past missions that forged Doc and the others into such a close, effective team and anchored the president's immense confidence in them.

"If you ask me, those questions are just a bunch of rabbit holes," Q said dismissively.

"That's because you're not a hopeless romantic, Q," Madeleine said as gently as she could. "You're a man of action, like Doc. You quickly move on from questions that don't demand answers, like a craftsman who discards tools he doesn't use, like a warrior who carries only the weapons that serve him well.

"But if and when people learn of the things our team has done and become intrigued with how we accomplished them, they will want to read as much about the team as they can. For them, the Grand Mysteries will add color and texture to the big picture of who we are. For students of history, the stories of where our missions took us, the roads we traveled, the paths we followed, and the trails we blazed will be important, of course. But they'll be made more alive by the accounts of the paths we didn't—or couldn't—follow and the corners we chose not to turn."

"I've never looked at what we do in quite that way, Madeleine," Doc conceded. "So now I understand why you walked away from your work at the Vatican library and insisted on going with me to search for the lost treasure of the Knights Templar."

"Well, it only took you three whole years to figure that out!" Madeleine poked at him.

"Connie would tell you that's pretty quick for me," Doc said with the grin she'd hoped for.

"Well, I must admit, I only *hoped* it would be true when Louis and I left Rome with you, Doc," Madeleine told him. "I remember how upset you were to have to take me along to Israel," she chuckled. "And at the time, I thought of it merely as having won an argument, as having proved my point. But that all changed when we met Julienne Artimus LaDevereux. Do you remember what you said about him?"

"Not exactly," Doc answered.

"You said he was not a man," Madeleine reminded him, "that he was 'something else entirely.' And in all the time since, have you given any thought to how it was that we spoke with a Templar Knight who claimed to be more than 700 years old?"

"Not really," Doc said flatly. "We could never know for sure anyway."

"Exactly! That was our first Grand Mystery, Doc," she said simply. "It's the sum total of all the questions we had as we stood before him and then as we watched him vanish into thin air. Finding him there made us certain we were close to the treasure. But that was all we really knew about him, and it's all we'll ever know. That's what makes the mystery grand and transforms that mission into a high adventure for those who will someday read about it.

"On our next mission, you discovered that Jonah Baird was 'the Keeper.'" Madeleine continued. "But we never learned why he chose that name. But more important, why did he create 'the Forbidden Library'? Why does he call the militia that serves him in his criminal enterprises the Guardians? How many are there? And how does he control them?

"And this current mission may very well have the most Grand Mysteries yet!" Madeleine said. "Why is Legionnaire Gabriel Chastain convinced he's Nostradamus, of all people? Are any of his so-called prophesies genuine? If so, what's their origin? And if Chastain truly believes he's Nostradamus, where does he think he's been for the past 500 years—and what does think he had been doing?

"We may never learn the answers to those questions," Madeleine told Doc. "And while they're not likely to prevent us from completing our mission, they add intrigue and food for thought that might very well fascinate and stoke the imaginations of readers for generations."

"What was I thinking when I didn't want you on the team!" Doc asked, shaking his head.

"Now *that's* the Grandest Mystery of them all!" Madeleine said with a big, bright smile.

"I don't know about anyone else, but all this conversation's made me sleepy," Q said. "I' headed in. Good night folks!"

"I'm right behind you, Q," Doc said and led the rest of the team back into the barracks to get some sleep before their morning flight to D.C.

Doc walked Jenny and Louis to their room to say goodnight.

"Louis and I still have so much to learn about this team, Doc," Jenny said. "Madeleine's review of the Grand Mysteries just scratched the surface for us. Our hope is that most of the questions on our list *have* answers…and that we learn them in due time. I'm sure you will," Doc said with a knowing smile, "especially with Madeleine on the team!"

After saying goodnight to the Marine couple, Doc stopped at the door to Noah and Madeleine's room and knocked lightly. Madeleine opened it just enough for her face.

"Forget something, Captain Holiday?" she asked him affectionately.

"Nope," he said quietly. "I just want to ask you a question I hope never makes your list of Grand Mysteries."

"Which one is that?" she asked with interest.

"Where in the world will Baird and Chastain go next?" Doc asked, in case she had a clue.

"Well, I admit I haven't a clue where they might go. But don't you dare let it keep you awake," she sighed. "Just remember what you always say, 'Everything happens for a reason.'"

Then she kissed the fingers on her right hand and pressed them to Doc's left cheek.

"Goodnight, Doc," she said affectionately and softly closed the door.

## 14

## "DEAD OR ALIVE" IN ANY LANGUAGE

The next morning, about the time Rafe and "the Dozen" piled into the SUVs inside a secure hangar at Joint Base Andrews for the trip to the White House, Baird poured Chastain a cup of coffee he'd brewed over the campfire. The pair settled onto large rocks to enjoy their coffee, and Baird began spinning a web of lies he hoped would answer the questions he knew the man who called himself Nostradamus must have about the attack the day before —and the time that was missing from his memory.

"Why are they so determined to capture us?" Chastain asked the obvious first question.

"Evil government forces envy our power," Baird began spinning his web of lies. "They resent my control of a well-trained, dedicated army of fearless soldiers, and they covet your power to know the future. But thankfully, you put up a remarkable fight yesterday, Nostradamus," Baird continued. "You weren't quite yourself after being hit by whatever they fired at us. But we'd all be goners if not for you!"

"I can't remember a thing after being hit by that blast," Chastain said. "That was an amazing weapon they used on me. But I overcame it, just as I overcome all adversity! I don't know where we are now or how we got here. But I'm glad I was able to help make our escape."

"That you did!" Baird did his best to puff up his new partner and avoid having to provide details he hadn't made up yet.

"So, where are we?" Chastain asked.

"We're in the Black Mountains of Arizona, near the Nevada border," Baird told him. "You led us here. Don't you remember that either?"

"I don't," Chastain replied uneasily. "I've never been here before."

"But you told us you knew it would be safe here, and you were right," Baird continued to lie. "Your powers of prophecy saved our skins! How amazing it is that you see what is unforeseeable to others the way you do!"

Ironically, Chastain didn't see Baird's false praise for what it was. Though his affliction apparently enabled him to see the future, it blinded him to the fact that Baird was using him. So he focused on the day ahead.

"So, where do you plan to go from here?" he asked

Baird in the hope that the mad man was not looking to him for what to do next.

When Chastain asked the question, Baird was relieved to see that his lies had put a smile on the AWOL Legionnaire's ruggedly handsome face. He knew his tale had worked—at least for the short run. Chastain's question also informed Baird regarding the limits of his partner's prophetic powers. Though his prophecies were often significant, each was like a stepping stone into the future. Yet, like everyone else, Chastain could not predict what would occur in the time between each step.

"We're going on a very important trip," Baird told him. "I want to show you the site I've selected for my new Forbidden Library. I believe you will find it to be a worthy repository for your priceless scrolls."

"But I still don't have the means to recreate them," Chastain told Baird, the first of several lies about the scrolls. "I failed to retrieve the flash drive before we were interrupted in Sedona. And I fear it won't be safe to return there for some time."

"Is it safe where you left it?" Baird asked.

"No one will find it," Chastain told the veiled truth.

"Then we'll let it be for now. In the meantime, there's much to do to ready the library. I'm certain you'll be impressed with the vision I have for it. Once we've prepared it, we can return and safely retrieve and preserve the flash drive in its proper historic context.

That will ensure your legacy of predicting historic events that have yet to happen.

"Once the flash drive is secured, we'll have all the time we need to reproduce the scrolls on the very same parchment as the originals. I cannot tell you how proud I will be to add those historic documents to my collection. The Forbidden Library will be my crowning achievement, and your scrolls will be the brightest gem in that crown!"

"I first conceived of my Forbidden Library to protect the world from offensive, evil and undeserving works of evil writers and artists," Baird told his wary partner. "But the addition of your marvelous work will elevate the library's mission to an eminence even I did not originally conceive. It will shine for all time as the bright, beautiful source of truth in the midst of the many dark, grotesque works of far-lesser mortals of our time."

Baird pulled out all the stops in his bid to perpetuate Chastain's delusion of being Nostradamus of the 16th century.

"And most important," the evil billionaire pronounced, "it will ensure future generations will appreciate the power of your prophecies. So you must begin thinking about what you will call the collection. Your first collection, *Les Prophéties*, is a landmark historic work. And I'm convinced your latest work will be even more important for centuries to come!"

While the Guardians broke camp and prepared for the

chopper Baird had sent for, the severely traumatized, schizophrenic man who called himself Nostradamus was proud that he had once again eluded capture and gotten the best of adversaries he considered to be inferior. Of course, Rafe and the president's "Dozen" were anything but inferior. Quite the contrary, they possessed the highest order of ability, courage, and tenacity: the essential traits needed to bring Baird down and bring Chastain in. They had readily accepted the mission to capture Chastain and return him—and his scrolls—to France. They knew it was an extremely dangerous mission, given the Legionnaire's highly trained, hair-trigger lethality and his alliance with the treacherous and equally lethal Jonah Baird.

During the flight back to D.C., the team discussed what they knew thus far. Doc wanted to be sure of a number of things before briefing the president on the events in Arizona—and hearing what the White House knew about the Camp David attack—mainly, how the Guardians knew Connie and Marsha were there.

"It pains me to admit it, Doc," Q began the discussion, "but we don't know much. We can't even say that Chastain really believes he's Nostradamus. Rafe stunned Chastain just moments into the assault at Devil's Bridge. And I'm not convinced that explains why the AWOL goofball was suddenly himself again. For all we know, it may all be an act to avoid answering for his crimes."

"The Gabriel Chastain I know would never go AWOL. Nor would he masquerade to avoid the consequences of his actions!" Rafe quickly replied. "The man I know is the warrior who saved my life in that cockpit."

"So you're convinced, Chastain really is afflicted with trauma and PTSD and that your stun gun somehow brought him out of his delusion?" Doc asked for the record.

"Without a doubt!" Rafe answered abruptly.

"Well then, we'd better hope that the effect was only temporary and that your friend has relapsed and again believes he's Nostradamus," Doc said. "Without the ability to predict the future, he's of no use to Baird. And if he has no memory of the where he hid the scrolls, he cannot help the U.S."

"None of that matters to me or to France," Rafe declared. "My mission remains the same."

"As does ours," Doc agreed, "at least until we know more. So until then, we're still in this together and committed to finding Chastain and his scrolls no matter the cost."

"Well, I'll tell you what I know," Q said when his patience with the speculation had run out. "I know my gut tells me those two are just a couple of conmen who are conning each other. Doc, we both know Baird, and we also know the so-called fortune-teller is in way over his head."

"I can understand your feeling that way, Q," Doc conceded. "And whatever the facts are, we all know there's no time to lose if we're going to succeed at bringing them both to justice. And we don't even know where to look next. We've still got almost three hours in the air, and I don't want to arrive at the White House as uncertain of the facts as we are right now."

Doc grabbed the encrypted phone from its charger and hit the White House speed dial.

"Hello, Captain Holiday," Camilla Renfro said in her friendliest voice.

"Hello, Camilla," Doc replied with a smile. "There's no surprising you, is there?"

"Not over the president's private line," Camilla chuckled. "He's in another meeting at the moment. Can I take a message?"

"We're headed into D.C. for a face-to-face in about four hours, right after Q and I see Connie and Marsha at Walter Reed," he said. "But I was hoping to have just a few minutes with him before we arrive," Doc told her.

"Yes, you're on his calendar this afternoon," Camilla confirmed. "He's supposed to welcome a group of foreign exchange students for a tour of the White House right after this meeting, but I'll corral him when he comes out of this meeting in about ten minutes and put the call through to you. Stay near the phone."

"Roger that...er, I mean, I will," Doc said as he

chuckled at the slip. "Thanks, Camilla. You're the greatest!"

"Roger that!" Camilla said with a laugh.

"Follow me," Doc said simply to the team after ending the call.

He led the others into the theatre room and settled into one of the luxurious leather Louis Vuitton reclining chairs with the phone cradled in his lap. The others settled in too and spun their chairs to face him.

"The president will be on the line in a few minutes," he told them. "What do we need to know before we land?"

"Does he have any idea where they've gone?" Jenny started the list of questions.

"Are they just on the lam, or are they headed somewhere for a particular reason?" Q asked. "And after he answers that one, I have a doozy for him."

"What might that be?" Doc asked hesitantly.

"How in the hell did the Guardians know Marsha and Connie were at Camp David?" Q shot back. "Is there a mole in the White House?"

"You took my question," Doc sighed. "And I suspect he knows it'll come up."

"He should!" Q almost shouted. "He better have an answer too!"

"What did you mean by 'on the lam,' Q?" Rafe asked.

"Running away, on the run," Q answered.

"In French, it's 'en fuite,'" Rafe told him.

"Well, however you want to say it, I'm tired of chasing Baird around the globe, and always being a step behind him," Q said in frustration. "At this point, I just want to hear the president tell us to bring him in dead or alive… and I don't care what language he says it in!"

Rafe was sure that hearing only Doc's end of his conversation with President Prescott would do little, if anything, to alleviate his concern with Doc's priorities for the mission. That realization made it clear to Rafe that he should find another seat far enough away to avoid overhearing it. It also triggered another, even more important, realization: Since their reunion, he hadn't done anything to alleviate Madeleine's sadness and hurt over his long, mysterious estrangement from their family…most especially from her, his once greatest and dearest friend and champion.

Rafe was a little out of sorts when his search for a more comfortable place to sit led him to an empty seat next to Madeleine, who had lost herself in the view of the pre-dawn Arctic sky outside the window beside her seat. Despite his well-documented heroics, the Legionnaire slid into the seat beside his younger sister with more than a little nervousness and trepidation. He knew her heart and mind struggled to contain the hurt and anger caused by his sudden and long disappearance without a clue regarding his motives.

"What's up?" Madeleine asked him with eyes wide as he settled in beside her.

That simple question, and her undeniable surprise at his having sat next to her, put a lump in his throat.

"Nothing's up," he began simply enough. "I just wanted to spend some time with you while we have it."

"We could have had *years*, Alexandre," Madeleine said with a tinge of resignation. "What makes you want to spend what little time we may have left with me all of a sudden?"

"I suppose I deserve that," Rafe replied sadly.

"Oh, there's no doubt in my mind, big brother!" Madeleine said more loudly than intended. "Do you have any idea how much confusion and hurt you caused by leaving so suddenly without a word of where you were going, or why?"

"Whether right or wrong, I had my reasons, Madeleine," Rafe said softly and touched her hand, only to have her jerk it away.

"*Oh really?*" Madeleine asked incredulously. "I remember trying to convince you not too long ago that everything happens for a reason. So now *you* can try to convince *me!*"

"Do you remember, Joanna?" Rafe asked quietly and swallowed hard.

"Of course!" Madeleine said indignantly. "She was wonderful. Mother and Father loved her immensely, and she treated me like a little sister…until the day you left, and she stopped visiting. It wasn't until months after her death that we had any idea what had become of her. She thought the world of you, Rafe. As young as I was, I could tell she was in love with you. How could you discard her so callously? What could possibly have gotten into you to walk away from her—and from your family without a word or even a goodbye?"

"Do you know how Joanna died?" Rafe asked even more quietly, with a tear in his eye.

"How could I?" Madeleine asked in response. "She had no family. It wasn't until she stopped visiting that we realized how little we really knew about her. She was a private person."

"*Very private*," Rafe replied, even softer yet. "But I loved her dearly, Madeleine."

"The truth is, you treat those you love very badly, Rafe!" Madeleine held nothing back.

"You have no idea," Rafe said with a shudder as he held back tears. "I loved Joanna beyond measure. She was my world. I know I didn't show my true feelings for her around you and mother and father. But that was not an honest measure of the depth of the love I had for her."

"Oh, indeed!" Madeleine grew loud again. "The *honest measure* of your love was when you left her—and us!"

"*I didn't leave her, Madeleine! She died!*" Rafe finally told her.

"I know she died!" Madeleine shot back. "We learned it from a near-stranger, not you!"

"Do you know *how* she died?" Rafe asked hesitantly.

"We were told she had some kind of hemorrhage," Madeleine answered.

"She died on an abortionist's table," Rafe said and began to cry. "She bled to death in an effort to end a pregnancy she couldn't bring herself to tell me about."

"I don't understand?" Madeleine said in shock and confusion. "She loved you deeply. If you loved her as deeply as you say, why on earth would she have an abortion?"

"Because I had cavalierly and thoughtlessly said on a number of occasions that I wasn't sure I ever wanted to have the responsibility of raising children," Rafe struggled to say as he began to cry harder. "God forgive me, I can't even say I ever even gave the prospect of fatherhood any serious thought. I just flippantly tossed out there that I had given our parents such a challenge as a child that I wasn't sure I wanted to risk having to deal with parenting. God help me, Madeleine! I can't even say that I really meant it. I just treated the whole topic so cavalierly that my mouth engaged, but my brain never did!

"Oh, I was young and stupid. She and I both were. But I loved her more than life itself. I just never told her so. And what she didn't tell me was that she had become pregnant," Rafe said as he broke down and wept uncontrollably with his face in his hands. "I can only believe that she thought I would be angry—that I might leave her—if she told me. So in my selfish, mindless state of mind, I had unintentionally managed to communicate to a sensitive, loving woman with no family to call her own, that the last thing I wanted was a family. She confided in a woman she worked with at the dress shop and was given the name and address of a man who could 'fix her problem' with no one being the wiser.

"It wasn't until after I returned to the shop a half-dozen times enquiring about Joanna that the woman finally told me she had died during the abortion along with our daughter. Unable to face mother and father and you with the horrible truth of what had happened, I used what little money I had to move them both to a suitable grave with a fine marble marker. And there I will join them both one day. Then, more deeply hurt and ashamed than I can ever express, I joined the Legion and volunteered for whatever duty would take me far away from France."

"Where are they buried, Alexandre?" Madeleine softened and asked her brother gently.

"In the cemetery beside the church you and I were raised in," Rafe told her.

"Oh, my!" Madeleine gasped. "Is it the grave with the nameless marker near Mama's and Papa's graves?"

"That's it," Rafe admitted. "I've paid for our names to be engraved when I join them."

"Well, there's no need for secrecy anymore, big brother," Madeleine assured him. "So you must have their names soon. By the way, what did you name your daughter?"

"Madeleine Marie…" Rafe told her, and they quietly wept together.

"I love you, Alexandre," Madeleine said as she wiped her tears away and clasped his hands in hers.

"And I love you too, Madeleine," Rafe said solemnly and kissed her on the forehead.

## 15

## "IN THE BELLY OF THE BEAST"

Q had calmed down by the time the phone in Doc's lap rang.

"Hello, Camilla!" he said eagerly. "This is even sooner than I'd hoped."

"Hello, Captain Holiday," Camilla replied cheerfully. "The president's meeting wrapped up a bit early, and he wanted to speak with you asap. I'll connect you now. I'll see you shortly, Captain. Have a safe flight in!"

"Thank you, Camilla," Doc said.

"Hello, Doc!" the president said in his usual cheerful voice. "I take it something can't wait until you get here."

"I'm sorry to bother you, Mr. President," Doc said sincerely. "But as much as I hate to admit it, we're flying by the seat of our pants here. Baird and Chastain are on the run again, as you know, and since the Situation Room lost the ability to track their movements, we have no idea where they're headed. Absent that info, we're unable to formulate a plan. So I'm hoping your intelligence sources have briefed you regarding Baird's likely next move."

"As a matter of fact, I'm in the middle of shaking those trees and beating those bushes now, Doc," the president answered. "I'm unhappy to tell you it's been slow going here. Baird's devised ways to elude our tracking systems. His aircraft are either flying very low, or his forces have devised a way to cloak them. Bottom line: We're not at all sure where he is at the moment. There is a bright spot, however!" the president sounded cheerful again. "I'm awaiting analysis of a document the Secret Service found on one of the Guardians who had the extreme misfortune of crossing paths with Connie and Marsha at Camp David. I'm confident I'll have it by the time you arrive. It's written in a code we're having a difficult time unraveling. But I can tell you it has the look of a directional memo. So we're hopeful it will provide a lead regarding Baird's new destination. With luck, we'll have useful information to share when you arrive."

"I picked a winner for a wife, didn't I, Mr. President?!" Doc asked, happily.

"You certainly did, Doc!" the president agreed. "And Walter Reed has taken excellent care of her and Marsha while you and Q have been gone!"

"You have provided added security at the hospital, haven't you?" Doc asked warily.

"I've assigned two U.S. Marshals to stand watch right outside their door, Doc. I spoke with both of those amazing ladies by phone a little more than an hour ago, and they can't wait to see the two of you. I'm anxious to talk with you and the rest of your team myself! So I'll hang up and look forward to speaking with you all face-to-face shortly. Goodbye for now, Doc!"

"Goodbye, Mr. President. See you soon," Doc replied.

Noah, Louis, Madeleine, Jenny, and Rafe got comfortable in the hospital's main floor waiting room while Q and Doc went upstairs to see Marsha and Connie. Jenny broke out the deck of Uno cards with the "Prescott" logo that she "borrowed" from the president's plane.

Q took his Stetson off and began fumbling with it before the elevator doors closed. Doc knew that meant his friend was worried for Marsha despite reassurances from the president and attending physicians that she and Connie had only a few minor bruises and scrapes.

"You ready for that big smile Marsha always has for you, Q?" Doc asked his closest friend.

"I sure am," Q sighed. "I don't know that we did the right thing sending them to Camp David, Doc. And I sure need to know how the Guardians knew they were there."

"It was the right thing to do, amigo," Doc replied. "They were happy for the chance to be there. The attack needs to be explained. But for now, let's take a deep breath and make the most of their being okay and eager to see us."

"Roger that!" Q said with a weak smile but continued fumbling with his hat.

The elevator doors opened to the quiet hush of the third floor, where even the lighting was subdued. The relaxed vibe was a welcome change from the hustle and bustle of the main floor, and it immediately had a calming effect that Doc hoped would help Q relax. But he could tell by Q's fast walk that it didn't. Holding the biggest floral arrangements sold at the hospital's flower shop, they followed the wall signs around three corners and finally caught sight of two smartly dressed men leaning against a wall on either side of the doorway to W-314. The pair snapped upright and were all-business as Q approached them, several steps ahead of Doc.

"Good afternoon, Chief Deputy Marshall!" the older of the two sentries said as he shook Q's hand warmly. "I recognize you from photos at headquarters. It's an honor to finally meet you, sir. I'm Supervisory Deputy Daniel Walters, and this is Deputy Chris Jenson."

"Very pleased to meet you, sir," Jenson said. "I've heard a lot of inspiring stories about you, sir, especially the one about how you saved former President Gannon's life—how you performed CPR on him for nearly 20 minutes on the way to the hospital when the AED aboard the presidential limo malfunctioned."

"Well, that's quite a stretch of the facts," Q chuckled humbly. "It was more like ten minutes, and I just happened to be closest to him when he collapsed."

"He heard the story from me," Walters told Q, "and I heard it straight from Chief Deputy

Brett Reed, who was standing right beside you that day in Tacoma when the Secret Service boys all looked on like deer caught in the headlights. And he told me it *did* take nearly 20 minutes to get him to the hospital because of the crush of the crowd at the rally."

"Reed always was an exaggerator," Q replied with an impish smile. "But if you please, I'd like to see my wife now."

Q smiled broadly as he carefully maneuvered Marsha's big vase full of flowers through the doorway while still clutching his Stetson.

"Marsha, you look gorgeous!" Q announced loudly the moment he locked eyes with her.

Doc smiled when he heard Marsha gasp at the sight of her flowers.

"Thanks for the history lesson, fellas," Doc paused a moment and said to the marshals. "I never heard that story before."

"For the record, *it was almost 20 minutes,*" Walters assured Doc with a smile.

"Oh, my goodness! They're beautiful!" Connie

gushed when she saw Doc enter the room carrying a large, cut glass vase of long stem white roses, pink carnations, and multi-colored moth orchids. "They *are* gorgeous! But you two didn't need to do this."

"Speak for yourself, Connie!" Marsha chided her friend with a chuckle. "Men get medals for what we did! So there better be some gourmet chocolates in our future too!"

"It's wonderful to see that glorious smile of yours, Beauty," Doc told Connie softly as he sat on the edge of her bed and kissed her.

"President Prescott was kind enough to arrange for us to share this quiet room and to have two guards outside our door around the clock," she said. "Do you remember this room, John?"

"Are you going to tell me this is the room where I first laid eyes on you?" he asked as his eyes scanned the nondescript beige walls.

"It is!" she giggled. "Is that fate, or what?"

"Frankly, it's a coincidence I could live without," he replied.

"But since I'm here, it's really quite special to me," she said with the sparkle in her eyes that Doc loved."

"Connie, do I know everything about your condition?" Doc asked. "Are you truly okay?"

"I'm fine, John, really," Connie assured him. "So you can stop worrying."

As Doc and Q stood up to leave, a distinguished looking doctor quietly walked into the room with a smile on his face.

"I take it you are the husbands," he beamed and extended a hand to the pair. "I'm Dr. Daniels. I'm pleased to meet you, Captain Holiday and Marshal Marshall. And I'm happy to report that these are two very lucky ladies…and you both are very lucky men to have them."

"Keep that up, and we may not leave for a while, doctor," Marsha said with a laugh.

"To the contrary," the doctor said. "I'm here to let you know that I expect to release you both a little later this afternoon as soon as I see the results of the few final tests I'm waiting for."

"That's good to hear, Doc!" Q said enthusiastically. "Uh…not you, Doc. This Doc," Q said, looking at Doc and pointing to Dr. Daniels.

"On that note, I'd say you two should hustle over to that meeting you have scheduled," Connie said without mentioning the president with Dr. Daniels in the room. "Sounds like we may be ready to go by the time you can get back here."

"We won't be long," Q pledged, and he and Doc hustled

to rejoin the team on the main floor and then pile into the hulking black SUVs waiting outside.

"I've got to ask the five of you to please ride in the front vehicle," Doc said to the team. "I've got to speak with Q privately about something."

Q gave Doc a quizzical look when he heard him make the unexpected request. His immediate thought was that he must have said something out of line inside to the doctor, and Doc wanted to call him on it. So he braced himself as the two of them hopped into the back of the second SUV.

"So it was you who saved President Gannon!" Doc said to Q the moment they were alone in the soundproof rear compartment. "I read about that episode in that book written by retired Secret Service agent Walter Jameson. And I did hear President Prescott mention once that he was grateful you happened to be at the Tacoma campaign rally when he was Gannon's vice president. But I never gave it much thought until now. You helped change the course of history, Q. I'm genuinely impressed."

"Not really, Doc," Q argued. "Prescott assumed the Office of the President a few days later when Jameson stepped down on the advice of his physician. But it would have happened immediately if Gannon had died that day."

"But Gannon didn't die, thanks to you!" Doc pressed the

point. "And Prescott has said on a number occasions that he's eternally grateful for the advice and counsel he still receives from Gannon from time to time. Jameson devoted a whole chapter to the incident in his book, *In the Belly of the Beast*. His account quite clearly credits your fast action for saving Gannon's life—especially your refusal to give in to exhaustion when you discovered no one else in the limo knew CPR. Too bad he never revealed your name."

"Believe me, Doc," Q replied. "I prefer it that way. Jameson got into enough hot water over the things he *did reveal* about things that happened inside 'the Beast.' He's still battling the government in court over his having disclosed things he saw happen inside the presidential limo."

"So now I know how you came to be an attaché to President Prescott," Doc surmised.

"That day might have had a little to do with it," Q said, looking to the heavens.

"My God, I'm close friends with a national hero!" Doc said with only a tinge of humor.

"I don't know if *you* are," Q said as he placed a hand on Doc's shoulder. "But I sure am."

## 16

### SVALBARD (THE DOOMSDAY VAULT)

The team got the usual salutes and welcome outside the north entrance to the White House. Rafe, however, got special treatment from the Marines who stood watch there.

"It's good to see you again, Lieutenant Colonel Bellarose," the sergeant in charge said as all four leather-necks crisply saluted him. "Will French Ambassador LeCarre be joining you?"

"Not today, sir. And it's good to see you again too, Sergeant," Rafe replied as he returned an impressive salute of his own and hurried inside with the team, flanked by two of the marines.

"Hello, Q!" Camilla called out the moment the team stepped into the West Wing. "It's so good to see you all looking so full of energy," she said as she hit the intercom button and told the president the team had arrived.

President Prescott energetically opened the door to the Oval Office and threw open his arms to them.

"Welcome back!" he said. "Did you have a good flight and a good visit at the hospital?"

"Yes, and yes!" Doc replied with equal energy.

"Well, come on in and let's get as many questions answered as we can," the president said. "Where do you want to begin?"

"How'd the Guardians know Marsha and Connie were at Camp David?" Q asked bluntly.

"When the lot of you flew here, they put a tail on you and followed the SUVs all the way to the camp," the president said apologetically.

"And no one on the White House detail had a clue they were being followed?!" Q shot back incredulously.

"I'm deeply sorry it happened, Q," the president said sincerely. "We've upgraded our procedures already, and I can assure you that will never happen again. But I must also tell you that I am greatly relieved, impressed, and thankful—that your wives ultimately played key roles in repelling the attack. Frankly, without them, I doubt we would have had any hope of learning the whereabouts of Baird and the Legionnaire."

"You know?" Doc asked in surprise. "Where are they?"

"Since our mid-flight conversation, the Office of Naval Intelligence has deciphered enough of the note found on one of the Guardians Connie sent to the big Forbidden Library in the sky to be confident that Baird and Chastain are headed to Norway."

"Norway?!" Q bellowed. "Why would *anyone* go to *Norway*?!"

"Svalbard," the president said simply.

"Svalbard? What's Svalbard?" Q bellowed again.

"The global seed vault," President Prescott said, as if that explained everything.

"Svalbard island is part of a Norwegian archipelago in the Arctic Ocean, north of mainland Europe, about midway between continental Norway and the North Pole," Madeleine said as though everyone knew as much. "Actually, Svalbard is not part of geographical Norway but is an unincorporated area administered by a governor appointed by the Norwegian government. It's a special jurisdiction subject to the Svalbard Treaty, unlike Norway proper. In other words, Baird thinks he and Chastain are beyond our reach while he's there."

"Officially, diplomatically, he's right," the president said. "And to *really* complicate things, there are no roads connecting the seed vault to any of the nearest settlements, a little more than 25 miles away. Aircraft, boats, snowmobiles, and, of course, dogsleds are the only ways in or out. There's a small airfield about a mile away, but the terrain between it and the vault is impassable by anything other than dogsled or snowshoes most of the year—as it is right now.

"At any given time, a staff of roughly 100 scientists and support personnel from around the world live and work there," the president continued. "They're housed in a nearby, bare-bones village resembling a mining town of our 19th century wild west. They're all there because they want to be, and they're not at all prepared for the type of aggression Baird will introduce them to in order to take control of the facility."

"I don't get it," Louis said. "What possible use is it to him?"

"I've heard of seed vaults," Jenny said, "They're fairly common around the world. But I never heard of Svalbard...and I can't imagine what attraction it holds for Baird."

"It's most commonly called 'the Doomsday Vault,'" Madeleine explained. "It was conceived by American conservationist Cary Fowler and created through a partnership with the Consultative Group on International Agricultural Research in the first few years of this century.

"Carved out of solid rock in the side of a mountain, the vault officially opened in 2008 to preserve a wide variety of plant seeds that are duplicate samples, or 'spare' copies, of seeds held in gene banks worldwide. Its mission is to insure against the loss of seeds in other gene banks during large-scale natural or man-made global crises.

"Officially, the Norwegian government funded the $8.8 million construction cost. Any nation in the world can store seeds there free of charge. Norway and the Crop Trust pay for operational costs. Primary funding for the Trust comes from the Bill & Melinda Gates Foundation and other organizations and governments worldwide."

"Sounds like a lot of 1960's-style hippy 'Kum Ba Ya' to me," Q predictably commented. "Let's cut to the chase. What's Baird's interest in it?"

"According to the one Guardian who's talking to us, Baird plans to take the vault by force and turn it into his new Forbidden Library," the president said.

"That's not the Baird *I know*," Doc finally piped up. "It's way off the world's radar. Maniac that he is, he needs a place he can visit whenever it suits him—whenever he needs to bask in the murderous mayhem he's inflicted upon the world."

"That's my thinking exactly, Doc," the president said as he rose from behind his desk. "Follow me please for a glimpse of what our best strategic military minds are thinking."

The president led his "Dozen" and Rafe through a door in the Oval Wall they had no idea was there. On the other side of the door, the president opened elevator doors by placing his palm on a tablet-size screen embedded in the wall and allowing a laser to scan his left eye. The elevator doors opened silently, and the group stepped in. Moments later, the buzz of activity and huddles of conversations in the Situation Room ceased immediately as the president entered.

"Carry on!" the president said as he signaled a uniformed Naval officer to come down from a catwalk about a dozen feet from the ground.

"Welcome, Mr. President!" the fresh-faced officer said as he sprinted down the stairs.

"You're the voice on the radio!" Doc said.

"That he is!" the president said as he rested a hand on the fresh-faced officer's shoulder. "And he's a very capable voice to be in contact with in a pinch! Corporal Oliver, I'd like you to meet the most elite team of American patriots our nation may never hear about. I'll not introduce them to you for the sake of national security. But one day, you perhaps may be able to tell your grandchildren that such a group existed. And this is Lieutenant Colonel Alexandre Rafael Bellarose, of France's 2nd Foreign Parachute Regiment," the president said with a broad smile. "He's here in service to France, one of our nation's oldest and mightiest allies. If anyone asks you, you've never seen or heard of him. Understood?"

"Understood, Mr. President," the corporal said with utmost seriousness.

"Please initiate the Svalbard video in the screening room for us, if you would, Corporal," the president said in his usual comforting voice.

"Right away, sir!" the corporal replied and hustled off.

"Does he run all the time?" Q asked in his hopelessly dry humor.

"*All the time!*" the president played along.

President Prescott then led the group into a small theatre off the Situation Room and quickly took a seat so the group would feel at ease taking seats too. In moments, the lights went off and the screen came to life with a view of the ominous, dark gray, wedge-shaped concrete structure that disappears into the ground and serves as the entrance to the Doomsday Vault.

"That looks like something out of a Hollywood sci-fi movie," Louis said.

"I think you'll find the views of the interior beyond reality too," the president said.

For the next 15 minutes, the group got an overview of the interior of the structure, the labyrinth of long concrete corridors that connect dozens of large, nondescript rooms, each containing hundreds of rows of steel shelving upon which were organized seemingly endless boxes filled with seeds from around the world.

"It's easy to understand why the vault appeals to Baird," the president told the group as he rose to stand beside the screen. "Officially, the reinforced concrete structure is 11,000 square feet of engineering genius. Built inside a mountain, it's honeycombed with comfortable, modern offices and work areas to support a staff of about 100 scientists and technicians from around the world. Together, they oversee the vault, which has a constant interior temperature of about minus-20 degrees Celsius. The heating, cooling, and ventilation system is engineered to adapt the environment of the complex in the event of an environmental catastrophe outside the vault."

"You said 'officially,' Mr. President," Doc noted. "So, just how big is it *really*?"

"Just under 50,000 square feet," the president replied with a smile. "And yes, we know that because we were unofficially involved in its construction."

"So what else is housed there…unofficially?" Rafe asked.

"That's an area I'm not at liberty to discuss," the president said. "But it's irrelevant to our discussion and purpose. The point is that Baird is either headed to or has already arrived in Svalbard, and there's plenty of reason to worry about what his intentions are."

"Give us some perspective, please, Mr. President," Madeleine asked of him.

"The vault's significance goes far beyond its contents," President Prescott told them. "The archipelago has a warmer climate than other areas at the same latitude. It's a breeding ground for many seabirds, and is home to polar bears, reindeer, the Arctic fox, and many marine mammals," the president continued. "Seven national parks and twenty-three nature preserves cover two-thirds of the archipelago, protecting the largely untouched, fragile environment. So I don't have to tell you the international chaos Baird would cause if he were to take the vault over and hold it for ransom like he planned to do with the lost A-bombs you folks helped ensure he never got his hands on. There's no telling how much the international community might be willing to pay for Svalbard's liberation, and the last thing Baird needs is more money to subsidize his madness."

"What lost bombs is he talking about?" Rafe quietly asked Doc.

"Let that go," Doc told him. "Q and I will bring you up to speed on it if and when you need to know."

"Roger that!" Rafe replied.

"This guy's more American every day," Q softly chuckled in the background.

"So now that we know where we're headed, what *exactly* is our mission?" Doc asked.

"We knew our mission back in Arizona," Q said cynically. "Put an end to Baird's madness by any means necessary."

"But each of you must remember that Legionnaire

Gabriel Chastain is with him," the president quickly added. "And returning him safely to France is mission-critical."

"Thank you for your fidelity, Mr. President," Rafe said.

"By all means, Colonel," the president assured him.

"*Lieutenant Colonel*," Rafe gently corrected the president.

"Well, I'm confident you'll be a full colonel by the end of this mission," the president replied with a wink and a smile.

"Sounds as though you're into prophecy too, Mr. President," Rafe replied.

"I assure you my thoughts about the future have a historical perspective. From what I know, you've had an amazing career. And getting your fellow Legionnaire safely back to France could very well be your crowning career achievement."

"I would be, as far as I'm concerned," Rafe replied.

"That's why President DuPris and I know you're the right man for this mission," the president said. "Once we have Legionnaire Chastain in custody, any additional success will, of course, be welcomed by me."

It wasn't lost on Doc and the other members of the team that the President didn't take issue with Q's interpretation of their mission. So he gave Q a subtle nod and a knowing look.

"I have only two requests, Mr. President," Doc said next. "Q and I must be at Walter Reed when our wives are released shortly. And with all this attention to safety, Q and I must be certain that you can ensure their safety until we complete this mission."

"Vehicles are parked right outside, waiting to take you both back to Walter Reed, Doc," the president said. "And I promise you that Connie and Marsha will be the very special guests of Melania and me in our personal residence, here at the White House until you return. How's that?"

"Perfect, Mr. President! Thank you!" Doc answered.

"Yes, thank you, Mr. President!" Q added with a look of relief.

"So when do we leave?" Doc asked the president.

"The moment you can," the president answered. "A C130's being prepped and fueled at Andrews and your weapons lockers are being loaded onto it as we speak."

"Roger that!" Doc said and led the team back to the elevator behind the president.

Forty minutes later, Q and Doc pushed their wives in wheelchairs to the Suburbans waiting at the hospital's Emergency entrance. Secret Service vehicles cordoned-off the adjoining streets for several blocks to ensure the team's safety. They were impossible to miss with their brilliant blue LED tactical emergency lights flashing.

"I see security's been upgraded significantly," Connie said to Doc as he climbed into the SUV's back seat beside her.

"We're not taking any more chances, Beauty," Doc told her. "The Camp David attack taught everyone a lesson —including the president."

"I'm glad to hear that!" Marsha said and reached back over her shoulder to touch Q's hand. "Did you happen to remember to bring those chocolates?" she teased him.

"I'm sure you'll like the ones they serve in the White House," Q told her.

"The White House?" Connie asked in surprised confusion.

"You both will be the guests of the president and first lady until we get back," Doc told her and Marsha.

"Oh—my—goodness!" Marsha gasped. "I don't have a thing to wear!"

"Get your credit card out, Q," Doc laughed at his friend.

"Now dear," Q said softly, "President Prescott and his wife are really simple folks under all that pomp and ceremony. I'm sure whatever you've brought along will be just fine."

"In a pig's eye!" Marsha shot back. "Connie and I will take as many pictures with them as they'll stand still for.

And I'm not going to wear anything I currently own for any of them!"

"Better call the bank to have your credit limit raised, Q," Doc said, laughing even harder.

"Suddenly, you have a sense of humor!" Q told Doc in aggravation. "We'll see how funny you think it is when *your bill* arrives in the mail."

"How soon do you have to leave, John?" Connie asked in a return to seriousness as she stood up from the wheelchair at the SUV's rear door.

"Immediately, I'm afraid," he told her. "Baird's up to no good again, and the President wants us on top of him, pronto."

"You can't even spend one night at the White House with me?" Connie said with a pout.

"Not *this night*, Beauty," Doc replied. "But there will be other nights when I get back. I promise you."

"I'll hold you to that promise, darling," Connie said and kissed Doc deeply.

When the SUVs stopped outside the north entrance of the White House again, Doc and Q bolted out and helped their wives descend onto the cobblestone drive-way. They took just enough time to say sincere good-byes, told their wives they loved them dearly and that they were happy to deliver them to the First Family's residence safe and sound.

"I'll miss you more than ever, Marsha," Q told his wife softly and embraced and kissed her more sincerely than he had in quite some time.

"And I'll miss you, my knight in shining armor," Marsha said before one more hug and kiss.

"I'll be back before you know it, Beauty," Doc told Connie as he hugged her tight and kissed her deeply.

"That's impossible, and you know it, John," she replied between kisses. "Just come back to me the moment you can."

Both wives stood stoically on the steps of the north entrance and waved goodbye until they were sure the convoy could no longer see them. Rafe and Louis had transferred to Doc's SUV when Connie and Marsha stepped out. And they began picking Doc's brain just moments into the ride to Joint Base Andrews

"Rafe, I suspect you've had some demolition training," Doc queried.

"Quite a bit, actually," Rafe corrected him.

"Well, I assume that means you know a bit about reinforced concrete structures. Am I right?" Doc asked.

"That's a safe assumption," Rafe said with a grin. "But I'm no expert."

"All the same, I bet you have some understanding of the specs required to ensure the vault maintains steady air circulation and constant humidity levels as dictated by the contents of its various sections."

"You're getting out of my depth fast here, Doc," Rafe balked at taking too much credit.

"Then let's keep it simple," Doc replied. "It's safe to assume the vault has a security system and that the front entrance is sealed as tightly as Fort Knox. Correct?"

"Fort Knox?" Rafe replied with a lost look in his eyes.

"You're speaking English to a Frenchman," Q had to note at that point. "Keep it simpler."

"It will be impossible for us to walk in through the front door," Doc started over.

"Correct," Rafe replied.

"And we know there's no back door that anyone knows of," Doc continued.

"Correct," Rafe replied again.

"But somehow, somewhere, there has to be one or more openings through which fresh air flows into and out of the ventilation system, at some distance from the vault," Doc surmised.

"That suppose that's true," Rafe conceded.

"If it's so well-hidden that there are no photos of it, it might be unalarmed," Doc said.

"That *may or may not* be true," Rafe countered.

"Just go with it," Q encouraged the Legionnaire. "Doc's a great guesser."

"So I'm hoping you have some fancy French explosives in those weapons lockers you take everywhere you go," Doc said hopefully.

"That is *absolutely* true," Rafe replied with a wink.

"And there's no chance they can explode prematurely, right?" Q asked only half in jest.

"No chance, marshal," Rafe replied with another wink. "But don't get me upset."

An hour later, the team was headed to the Svalbard Doomsday Vault aboard the C130 at nearly 400 miles per hour, 30,000 feet up.

## 17

---

## DEAD SILENT

Thirty minutes into the flight, Noah settled into a seat beside Doc with a radio the pilot gave him at takeoff.

"Our friend, Corporal Oliver, wants to speak to you," he told Doc.

"The voice from the Situation Room?" Doc asked happily.

"The same!" Noah chuckled and handed Doc the radio.

"Hello, Corporal Oliver!" Doc said sincerely into the microphone

"Hello, Captain Holiday," Oliver replied. "I just wanted to assure you that the Situation Room is monitoring your team again, and you'll have our support as long as we can maintain contact once you're on the ground at Svalbard."

"Call me, Doc, please, Oliver," Doc requested.

"If you wish, Captain," Oliver said.

"I don't wish. I order you, Oliver," Doc said in pretend seriousness.

"Understood, sir...uh, Doc," Oliver stuttered.

"Loosen up, Oliver!" Q laughed heartily with the rest of the team. "You may be in D.C., but you're right here with us too—and we're glad of it! So welcome aboard young fella!"

"Thanks, Q!" Oliver said with a smile and a sigh of relief. "I'll try to remember that. The connection goes into 'Mute' mode after 30 seconds of silence. And it comes to life when someone at either end hits the 'Speak' button. You've got about a 16-hour flight ahead of you, Doc, with a mid-air refueling over Iceland. So plan accordingly and sweet dreams!"

"Hey, Oliver! While we have you on the line, does the Situation Room have a fix on the vault's ventilation exhaust system?" Doc asked.

"Not to date," Oliver answered. "Some here believe the system must not require one."

"Thanks, Oliver," Doc replied. "And thanks for being there. You will go home and get some sleep yourself before we talk again, won't you?"

"You bet, Doc," Oliver replied. "Talk to you somewhere beyond Iceland,"

"Roger that!" Doc said and put the radio under a cushion to talk with the team.

"Okay, team—here's what I'm thinking," Doc began to strategize. "If the U.S. helped finance construction of that place, I'd have to believe they'd know if it has the expensive space-age technology it takes to eliminate an exhaust port. So we're going to assume there is one and try to detect it before we land."

"How do we do that?" Noah asked.

"This buggy has Infrared Imagery capability," Doc answered. "If we can swoop in at 1,000 feet or less, I'd say we'll find it if it's there."

"Are you kidding?!" Jenny gasped. "How do we fly over at 1,000 feet or less without waking up the dead and announcing our arrival?"

"We'll have the pilot cut the engines and glide for one loop of the area," Doc answered.

"That'll be risky that far into the Arctic Circle," Rafe observed. "The engines might not restart. Then what?"

"Then we'll brace for a rough landing and hope Baird has a plane parked somewhere up there," Doc said with a forced smile.

"That's not funny, Doc," Q said.

"You're telling me!" Doc agreed, and the team quietly exchanged serious glances.

"Now, if you can, get some sleep," Doc said as he lowered the back of his seat and stretched out. "Talk to you all in about eight hours."

"There's a cramped shower in the bathroom," Madeleine told Jenny. "If you'd like to use it, I can wait."

"You're a saint, Madeleine," Jenny said with a look of relief.

"Just don't use all the hot water," Madeleine said with a smile. "Or I won't be so saintly."

Almost exactly eight hours later, Doc emerged as the last team member to shower and toweled his hair dry as he sat in the midst of the team.

"Good morning, everyone!" he said cheerfully. "I hope you all managed to get some sleep after hearing my plan before I said goodnight."

"We don't scare that easy," Jenny told him. "But all the snoring was a challenge."

"I don't snore!" Q protested so quickly and loudly it made everyone laugh. "Well, I don't!" he said again, more quietly.

"Maybe the frigid arctic air will cure any snoring tendencies among us before we head home again," Doc chuckled.

"I don't snore," Q mumbled one more time, and everyone laughed again.

"I'm not pointing a finger, Q," Doc chuckled.

"But if the shoe fits," Louis added to more laughter.

"What does that have to do with snoring?" Rafe asked innocently.

"Nothing at all," Louis dismissed the question. "Forget I mentioned it."

With that, Jenny again broke out the Uno cards, and the team pulled their chairs around her to be dealt in.

"I've never played this game," Rafe announced.

"Don't worry, Rafe," Jenny told him. "We've got plenty of time to teach you the game."

"Maybe we should call it 'Une' while a Frenchman's playing," Q suggested.

Jenny just ignored the suggestion and dealt the cards. As she did, Doc slipped up to the cockpit to talk with the crew. The co-pilot surrendered his chair to Doc and sat in a jump seat beside the engineer.

"Got something on your mind, Captain?" the pilot asked him.

"Since you've got my life in your hands, I'd prefer that you call me, Doc!" Doc told him.

"Okay, Doc," the pilot said and shook Doc's hand. "And you can call me Harm."

"Harm?" Doc asked with a raised eyebrow.

"It's short for Harmon," the pilot said with a smile. "My dad was a big Harmon Killabrew fan as a kid."

"Whew!" Doc chuckled. "For a minute, I feared you earned the name as a pilot."

"Call me Chuck," the co-pilot volunteered.

"And I'm Luther," the flight engineer said.

"Pleased to meet you fellas," Doc said. "How many hours have you got aboard C130s?"

"All together, I'd say about 1,000 hours," Harm quickly approximated. "Why?"

"I've got what might be a risky idea, and I need your input," Doc told the trio.

"We're all ears," Chuck replied.

"Is there a problem with turning the engines off over Svalbard and gliding at about 1,000 feet for one circuit over the area of the vault?" Doc asked, hopefully.

"Well, you're right about it being risky," Harm told him. "We'll arrive about 0500 hours, and the forecast we were given says to expect it to be around -30 degrees Celsius at that time of the morning. When you factor in the complication that the islands are the meeting place for very cold polar air from the north and mild, wet sea air from the south, we run the risk that the engines may not restart when we want them to. I mean, *when we need them to!*"

"So my idea's a bust," Doc shrugged.

"I didn't say that," Harmon hedged just enough to encourage Doc. "What's your reason for wanting to try such an unorthodox maneuver?"

"I know this ship has infrared imaging capability, and I'm hoping that if we can do a flyover at about 1000 feet, you might be able to detect the slightest hint of hot ventilation exhaust. *That* would allow us to access the vault undetected. But it's a moot point if they hear your Allison T56-A-16 turboprop engines two miles away. Instead, I want to glide in dead silent."

"That's an *excellent* reason to want to shut the engines down," Harm seemed to agree. "If it works, we could also do it as we swoop in to drop your team."

"So, you'll try it?" Doc asked just to be sure.

"What have we got to lose…besides one of the finest airships in the Navy's fleet?" Harm asked with an impish grin as Chuck and Luther high-fived each other. "We could shut one engine down and then restart it as a test. If it works, we'll be in a good position to risk all four."

"Thanks, guys!" Doc declared. "I know what I'm asking of you, and I'm proud to fly with you."

Doc gave Chuck his seat back and returned to the main cabin to stretch-out in a recliner and watch the "Uno" game from a distance while he formed a more-complete attack strategy.

The giant assault aircraft was still more than 1,000 miles away when Baird led Chastain on a grand tour of the vault they'd commandeered from its unsuspecting staff the day before.

"This vault offers us the opportunity to showcase your grand opus, Nostradamus," Baird told the Legionnaire and made sweeping arm gestures even larger than the lies he was spinning.

"Just how large is this structure?" Chastain asked.

"I'm not sure just yet," Baird admitted. "But I'm certain it's large enough to honor your greatest works, as well as conceal the world's most offensive productions for all time!"

"But who will take your place and keep it secure after you're gone?" Chastain asked.

"There's time enough to make those arrangements," Baird assured him. "And I have the financial means to underwrite it for centuries."

"Just how rich are you?" Chastain asked for the first time.

"Rich enough," Baird replied tersely. "And few rich men can honestly say that."

What Baird didn't say was that he had no intention of transforming the vault into his new Forbidden Library, but instead planned to ransom it for the funds that would cover the cost of duplicating it somewhere warmer and much more accessible to admirers he was sure he would someday have around the world. Baird kept that part of his plan to himself as he led Chastain into successive large concrete-lined rooms. Each contained row after row of steel shelving that rose from the floor to the ceiling, 20 feet above.

"This is grand!" he said excitedly. "It's perfectly lighted and ventilated to ensure the most perfect environment for its contents. The climate control is state-of-the-art. Well, that might not be quite accurate," Baird admitted. "It still relies upon conventional air quality control technology. But I have plans to upgrade that shortly."

The pair explored the vault's farthest known reaches for the next hour, then tired of the walking and headed back to the office area Baird had staked out after his Guardians rounded up the scientific teams and support personnel when they raided the vault before Baird and Chastain arrived there. Altogether, the Guardians zip-tied more than 100 unfortunate souls whose ultimate fate Baird still hadn't decided. They were consigned to a large room Chastain had not seen yet. Baird pondered that "detail" as he and the Legionnaire headed back to where their exploration began.

"Have we seen it all now?" Chastain asked him.

"Not quite all of it yet," Baird said cryptically. "But there's time enough tomorrow."

Baird very much wanted another day to decide the fates

of his captives. What he didn't know was that Doc and his team were headed his way to retake the vault.

With three hours in the air still ahead, Doc's eyes studied Rafe as the Legionnaire intently focused on the card game in front of him. Doc realized there was much about the French fighter he did not know. While the team was captivated by the cards before them, Doc quietly retrieved the radio and took it forward into the cockpit.

"Corporal Oliver, come in," he said quietly.

"Welcome back, Doc!" Oliver said cheerfully. "What's up?"

"Is it possible to transmit Lieutenant Colonel Bellarose's background file to me while I'm in the air?" he asked.

"Yes, sir!" Oliver replied. "I can have it to you in minutes."

"Make it happen!" Doc shot back happily.

Four minutes later, Luther handed the file to Doc, who returned to his recliner to review the particulars of Rafe's military profile. As brief as the profile was due to top secret constraints, it was still highly impressive,

**Name: Alexandre Rafael Bellarose**

**Rank: Lieutenant Colonel**

**Branch: Foreign Legion**

**Years of Service: 12**

**Commendations: Legion of Honor**

**National Order of Merit**

**Order of Maritime Merit**

**Medal for the War Wounded**

**Primary Role: Air assault**

**Specializations:**

- **Airborne Mastery**
- **Urban warfare**
- **Mountain warfare**
- **Desert warfare**
- **Amphibious warfare**
- **Demolition (land and marine)**
- **Sniping (King of 2 Miles - 2018)**

"King of 2 Miles?" Doc asked in his head. "What the heck is the King of 2 Miles?"

"Hey, Q," Doc called out. "Have you ever heard of something called 'King of 2 Miles'?"

"Yeah," Q replied without looking up from his cards.

"It's an impossible sharpshooter competition for gun nuts and fools—people crazy enough to think they can consistently hit a target less than two feet square from two miles away."

Doc found it revealing that Rafe never so much as looked up from his cards while Q made harsh statements about one of the Legionnaire's many remarkable achievements. Doc pondered what it might say about the man from France. It might say he had his performance and priorities in their proper perspective. It could also say that he didn't place much value on either. Or it could just say that he was so engrossed in the card game that he never heard Q's comments. Doc was eager to learn which it was. So he vowed to pay closer attention to the Legionnaire in the hours ahead.

# 18

## FATHER OF THE FUTURE

Q soon tired of the card game, and his eyes wandered about the cabin. He saw Doc pull something out of a compartment built into the wall of the fuselage and left the game for a closer look. As he approached Doc, the former SEAL team commander unfurled a large, round, heavily padded canvas bag about seven feet in diameter and spread it out on the cabin floor.

"What have you got there, Doc?" he asked

"It's a drop bag like I used back in the day," Doc replied as he unzipped it.

"What do you drop in those things?" Q asked innocently.

"Yourself and a weapon, usually," Doc said as he examined the bag's interior.

"You're kidding, right?" Q asked hopefully.

"No kidding, Q," Doc answered. "We dropped from choppers onto soft-packed sand."

Knowing Q would follow him, Doc sat in one of the high-back reclining chairs and looked out a window at the endless miles of snow below. Q quickly sat in the chair beside Doc.

"So why are they aboard a C130?" Q asked, fearful of the answer.

"Well, the snow's about four feet deep at Svalbard this time of year, and it should be much softer than sand," Doc replied. "So the bags will stop rolling sooner…if they roll at all."

"Now I *know* you're kidding!" Q said desperately. "There must be an airstrip there."

"Oh, I'm quite serious, Q," Doc assured him. "There's an airstrip, alright. But it's not long enough for a C130. When that card game breaks up, I'll brief everyone on the plan."

"I can hardly wait," Q said sarcastically and headed back to the card game.

Back at the White House at about the same time, Camilla opened the Oval Office door, and the president's Chief of Staff Jasper Cornwall strode in for a brief face-to-face.

"Good afternoon, Jasper!" President Prescott bellowed

as he stood up from his desk. "It's good to see you. We so seldom have the chance to talk privately.

"I couldn't agree more, Mr. President," Cornwall replied.

"So what's the special occasion?" the President asked.

"I received a letter this morning containing quite an unusual request from a constituent," Cornwall said. "And I thought we should discuss it so that I can draft an appropriate reply."

"What's the request, and who is it from?" the president asked with a curious expression.

"Retired Navy Captain Augustus Baird asked for a brief, private, off-the-record meeting with you here at the White House at your convenience," Cornwall told him.

"Really?!" the president asked, surprised and curious. "Well, I'll be. Did he say why?"

"Only that it is a deeply personal matter and won't cost you or the American people any money," Cornwall said with a smile.

"His wife recently died, and they were childless," the president thought out loud. "Perhaps he just wants someone to talk to about it all. Lord knows he can't talk to his brother, Jonah, about *anything*. The good captain's just across the river in Alexandria. How's my schedule tomorrow?"

"The morning's packed." Cornwall had it memorized,

as usual. "But you have a few minutes here and there in the afternoon."

"Did he give his phone number?" the president asked.

"He did," Cornwall answered.

"Well then, try to set up a meeting for tomorrow in the map room," the president said. "And arrange a ride for him, too, please."

"Consider it done, Mr. President," Cornwall said and rushed out of the Oval Office.

Alone again, the president looked out the window toward the Rose Garden and pondered what the man whose brilliant Naval career he'd spared years earlier might want to ask of him.

In Svalbard, at about the same time, Chastain returned to the office he'd chosen to serve as his quarters inside the Doomsday Vault. Weary after the tour, he locked the door and dropped into a high-back office chair behind a plain, gray metal desk. As the 16th-century physician, apothecary, astronomer, and seer, Nostradamus, the injured and traumatized Legionnaire lacked the energy and stamina he'd had as the war hero, Gabriel Chastain. The battle in Arizona, the journey to Svalbard, and the tour of the vault had all drained him of every bit of energy.

The chair emitted a shrill creak whenever Chastain shifted in it. But it was quiet and very comfortable when he rocked all the way back in it and put his feet on the desk. He interlocked his fingers behind his head, took a deep breath and was about to close his eyes when they fell upon a laptop computer within arm's reach atop the desk. The discovery presented his first chance to review his scrolls since he'd saved them to the jump drive three months earlier in France.

Suddenly energized, Chastain opened the laptop and watched it come to life as he unlaced his left boot and extracted the jump drive. He excitedly inserted the drive into the USB port and clicked on the "Scrolls" folder with a heady anticipation of seeing his prized prophecies again. When he clicked on the folder, his 28 prophesies were cataloged before him. Chastain was intensely —some would say insanely—proud of his collection of predictions.

"I am the father of the future!" his wounded mind told him. "Only I foresee events before they are born into the light of day and become known to lesser men! Many of my visions of the future have come to pass exactly as I say they will. They are a testament to the accuracy of my prophetic visions. Though the fools of the world scoff, a growing number of believers—many in positions of great authority and influence—understand and covet the power contained in the prophecies I have chronicled in these scrolls!"

As he was about to open one of the files, Baird knocked on the door and called out to him.

"Sorry to interrupt you, Nostradamus!" Baird shouted. "But I need to see something!"

"Can't it wait until I've had some sleep?" he asked hopefully.

"It cannot," Baird said flatly. "Once you see what I'm about to show you, you'll be happy I insisted that you follow me now and sleep later."

Chastain slowly stood up from the chair, unlocked the door, and let Baird in, but then remembered his left boot was untied. So he lowered himself onto the cot along the wall not far from the desk and discovered it was even more comfortable than the chair.

While Chastain tied his boot, Baird saw the open laptop on the desk. But it was turned away from him, and he had no idea Baird's prophecies were displayed on the screen. Sleepy as he was, Chastain didn't think to turn the laptop off and take the jump drive with him before he followed Baird out of the office and closed the door behind him.

As Baird led Chastain through the vault's stone-carved corridors, the card game aboard the C130 began to bore Rafe. He was focused on making sure Doc understood that Chastain's safe return to France was, as President Prescott had characterized it, "mission-critical." So he quietly slid into the seat Q had just vacated beside Doc with a dead serious look on his face.

"What's on your mind, Rafe?" Doc asked, but knew.

"Before the shooting starts, I need to be sure you understand that my primary mission is to find Gabriel and ensure his safety," he told Doc without blinking. "Once that's accomplished, I'll be at your command—ready, willing, and able."

"I understand completely and expect nothing less," Doc replied. "In fact, I hope you give him another blast with your PHASR pistol the moment you find him. Having seen him in action, I know it will be to our great advantage if he awakens as himself again."

"But I plan to remove him from the battle completely," Rafe pressed the point.

"If your fellow Legionnaire awakens as himself, I suspect it will not be easy to keep him from the battle," Doc predicted, "especially once he realizes *you're* in it."

"I've brought handcuffs with me, and I'll use them if necessary," Rafe vowed.

"Do what you will," Doc said with a faint, knowing smile. "I know your friend is extremely resourceful. I've seen what that soldier is capable of, and I'm confident his—and our—survival will be more certain with him in the fight."

"Be that as it may," Rafe hammered his point, "my mission is to save him, not enlist him."

"Roger that!" Doc replied with meaning as he led Rafe back over to the card game.

"Don't get up just yet," Doc said to the team as Jenny tucked the UNO cards back into their box, and he and

Rafe pulled folding chairs into the circle. "We need to discuss the plan."

"Wait until you hear *this*," Q told them while shaking his head. "This is better than anything that ever came out of one of those cans marked 'Worms' that we usually get."

"Well, if it came out of Doc's mind, I'm sure it's every bit as challenging," Noah said.

"Thanks—*I think*," Doc replied. "The success of this mission depends on the element of surprise. You know Baird's Guardian army is a band of suicidal mercenaries with a fanatical loyalty to a man they know is a cold-blooded killer. That formula alone makes this a very dangerous assault. The fact that they are hunkered-down in a concrete-lined bunker carved into a mountain more than 100 miles inside the Arctic Circle makes this the toughest assignment we've ever undertaken. But I know none of us has come this far to fail."

"You can say that again!" Louis replied. "We're all ears, Doc. What's the plan?"

"I told the president we would need the very best fire-power available and he didn't let us down," Doc began his list of weapons. "I only wish each of you had been given time to familiarize yourselves with the firepower you will bring to this fight," Doc said sincerely. "But I believe you have enough training with unconventional weapons to adapt quickly.

"We've got about two hours to get ready. So strap on your sidearms now. We'll carry strategic weapons as well. Rafe, I'll leave it for you to decide which of your weapons are appropriate for the plan I'm about to layout. But be sure to bring your PHASR pistol."

Doc then opened the weapons chest and began lifting out the munitions one-by-one.

"Each of us will carry a PHASR rifle strapped to our backs. But do not—I repeat, *DO NOT*—fire it prior to beginning our exit from the vault. Guardians you stun will only be unconscious for about 20 minutes, and I don't want any of them waking up between us and our exit point, understood?"

"Understood!" everyone but Rafe replied.

"If and when you *do* fire it, be sure to have the shielding glasses in place," Doc added. "I'll hand them out with the PHASRs. Put them on your heads now. I can assure you there will not be time to carry you out of the vault.

"I've also got bulletproof vests for each of us," Doc told them and passed them out. "They're from Poland, with love—made of light-weight 'Shear-Thickening Fluid' technology, which is lighter and stronger than Kevlar," Doc said. "It's also way more expensive, which is why you never heard of it until now. The vests are designed to fit over our parkas. In the middle of the back of the vest is a large pocket with a Velcro flap," Doc said and held up a small, plastic box resembling a large laptop battery. "In that pocket, you also have one of these," he said.

"What do we need a battery for, Doc?" Q asked with a bit of skepticism.

"This is no battery, Q," Doc replied as he gave the box a single firm shake, and it transformed into a stream-lined machine gun. "This is a prototype FMG-18, an extremely compact, light, polymer-based folding machine gun," Doc said. "Each has a 30-round clip of 9mm cartridges and two extra clips, which are in the pocket along with the weapon. In addition, you will each carry an M16 with four 40-round clips of SS109 cartridges, which you will wear on a belt around your waist. Q and I will each also carry one of these," Doc told the team and lofted a stubby automatic weapon that looked more like a stovepipe than a rifle.

"Kinda looks like a miniature bazooka," Rafe commented.

"It's an M25 Counter Defilade Target Engagement System. But our Special Ops forces affectionately call it 'the Punisher.' The calibrated explosive charges it fires silently travel through open doorways, windows and over walls—our between rows of shelves like those in the vault—then explode behind the enemy, wounding or killing them."

"I'm all for that!" Q chimed in.

"One more thing," Doc added. "Louis, you will carry

this MAHEM on your back instead of a PHASR, in case we need to blast through reinforced concrete."

"Roger that!" Louis barked in response.

"Well, President Prescott certainly delivered the firepower," Jenny said.

"We're done playing with this bunch!" Doc said, almost angrily. "I plan to walk out of that vault with mission accomplished. But I also want to stress that the vault is still packed full of seeds from many nations. So use all possible caution when we engage Baird and his Guardians. But at the same time, we must quickly gain the upper hand to ensure Baird does not have an opportunity to destroy the vault and everything in it."

"Including us!" Q said with a devilish chuckle.

"Any question?" Doc asked.

"Yeah," Rafe replied. "Are those drop bags on the floor?"

"I hoped someone would ask that," Q interjected before Doc could answer.

"They are," Doc said flatly.

"I don't believe they've ever been used for a drop out of a C130," Rafe said. "I thought there were used only for drops out of choppers at far lower altitudes."

"That's correct," Doc agreed. "But our flight crew's been trained to execute a low-speed, low-altitude maneuver that will enable us to drop out of the rear cargo bay onto the soft-packed snow below, which the Pentagon says is at least four feet deep."

"And this maneuver will be like the unpowered pass over the vault at less than 1,000 feet the crew plans to execute prior to the drop?" Rafe asked with admiration for the flight crew.

"Roger that!" Doc responded.

"I've never jumped out of a plane without a parachute," Jenny said softly.

"*I've never jumped out of a plane!*" Madeleine said much louder.

"We'll all be fine," Doc took some liberty with that assurance. "It'll be like rolling off a log. When we drop, the plane will be 25 to 30 feet above the ground...I mean above the snow."

"That's still one heck of a log to roll off of," Q replied sarcastically.

"Trust me, Q," Doc replied. "Have I ever let you down?"

"Is that a trick question, or just a bad pun?" Q asked in a strained attempt to lighten up.

"Since you're being so negative, let's just drop it," Doc said flatly.

*"That's a really bad pun,"* Q shot back, not ready to let it go.

"ETA is T minus 40 minutes," Harm announced over the loudspeaker.

"Time to get ready to go to work," Doc said.

"Roger that!" Q barked back, abandoned his doubt, and followed Doc to the cockpit to prepare for the powerless loop over the vault in search of its ventilation exhaust ports.

"You two are just in time to witness history in the making," Harm said to them excitedly as he looked over his right shoulder and gave Chuck, his flight engineer, the nod to double-check the wind velocity and direction before starting the long descent to just 1,000 feet above the snow-covered mountain top plateau below.

"Conditions could not possibly be more ideal," Chuck announced. "In addition to that big, bright, beautiful full moon at our backs, there's a slight, east-to-west breeze of just a third of a mile per hour at 200 feet."

"To God be the glory!" Harm muttered and calmly leveled the plane out at 1,000 feet.

"Infrared imagery is booted-up and ready to go," Chuck confirmed.

"Shutting engine number one down on my mark," Harm announced. "Three, two, one," he counted down and flipped the engine's emergency shut-off switch and watched the eight-foot-long propeller come to a halt. "I will attempt to restart it in exactly five minutes, about how long an unpowered full sweep of the plateau would take for thorough infrared imaging," he said.

No one in the cockpit breathed for the next few, heart-pounding minutes.

"I will attempt to restart engine number one on my mark," Harm finally announced. "Three, two, one!"

"YES!" Doc shouted when the engine came back to life without so much as a sputter.

"Looks like we caught a break!" Harm said with a long exhale of breath.

"Now, if we can only find the exhaust ports," Doc said and shot a glance at Chuck.

"Infrared imaging is engaged!" Chuck announced right on cue.

Harm throttled up the big C130 to 385 knots, then shut the monster engines down one at a time, and the plane glided silently like a giant American eagle, 800 feet in the air. Doc and Q anxiously watched Chuck's IR imaging screen over his shoulders. The screen was blank for nearly three minutes, but then came alive with eight tightly clustered hot spots.

"There it is!" Doc shouted with excitement.

"Sure enough!" Q said and began to breathe again.

"I've locked in the coordinates," Chuck said. "You've got 'em now, Harm," he said, and Harm saw them appear on the screen in front of him.

"Locking them into navigation control now!" Harm announced. "I'm ready to take this bird lower whenever you're ready, Doc," he said confidently. "Say the word, and I'll coax it down as close as possible to 50 feet above the plateau, then I'll open the rear bay door as we approach the exhaust ports again."

"Roger that!" Doc told Harm with a smile. "Time to get in the bag, Q," he told his friend.

"Gives a whole new meaning to being 'in the bag,'" Q wisecracked.

"Chuck, will you do us the honor of pushing us out of the cargo bay?" Doc asked.

"Well, that's a request I'm not likely to hear ever again," Chuck chuckled. "I'm honored."

"Doc, this is probably a bad time to ask this, but how do we get home?" Q asked gently.

"The president ordered a Sikorsky CH-53E chopper into the air from the Latrar Air Station on Sweden's northern coast four hours ago," Doc told him. "It should arrive in less than two hours. So let's make fast work of this and be ready to great the Super Stallion when it sets down."

"Roger that!" Q barked.

"We're ready to go, Oliver!" Doc said into his radio microphone on his cheek.

"Roger that, Doc!" Oliver shot back. "Wish I could see you off in person."

"Sorry, but we can't wait for you to get here," Q quipped.

The trio then headed rearward to the cargo bay, and into what might someday become known as both, a new page in the history of warfare, and the dawn of a new era in aerial combat.

## 19

---

# THE DOOMSDAY ASSAULT

oc walked briskly to the threshold of the cargo bay and stood erect and silent beside the weapons chest with a stalwart expression. He was expressionless as he watched his team members assemble in front of him with their sidearms strapped on. Solemnly aware of the danger he was about to lead them into, he briefly met the gaze of each member of his team. Proud of their courage and mindful of his role as their leader, he silently recalled the "True North" creed he and his SEAL team recited before each mission.

*"True North is the compass deep within that guides me! It defines who I am as a warrior*
*and as a human being! It is my fixed point in a spinning world! It anchors me!*
*It is my value and honor as a person, my strength and worth to my team!*

*No matter what decisions I must make, and actions I must take, True North tells me the way I must go!"*

Ready now, Doc opened the chest, handed out the weapons, and took command.

"Check your weapons, clips, and radios one last time, then grab a drop bag and fall in around me!" he ordered. "We've got less than ten minutes before this bay door falls open, and we begin our Doomsday assault! In a few minutes, I'll zip into my bag first so you can see how it's done! Then give each other space, turn on your helmet lights, and zip your bags shut around you! Secure the zipper using the clip that's clearly marked inside! Then pull the bright yellow tab that will be directly in front of you! That will inflate your bag, and you will become a human beach ball, seven feet in diameter!

"Chuck, our flight engineer, has graciously agreed to help us do something no one has ever done before," Doc told to the team. "So I guess you could say he's going to push each of us into the history books, if this mission is ever declassified, that is."

"Thanks, Chuck!" the team called out together.

"Proud to do it!" Chuck replied with a humble smile and an uplifted hand.

"You'll each have constant contact with me throughout the assault, and I will have contact with Corporal Oliver in the White House Situation Room until we penetrate the reinforced concrete of the vault! Can you hear me, Oliver?" Doc barked into his radio.

"I'm here, and I hear you loud and clear, Doc!" Oliver's voice was also loud and clear over the intercom and through each radio.

"Wish us luck, Corporal!" Doc told him.

"Good luck and Godspeed, team!" Oliver said proudly. "The president has asked me to tell you he's praying for each of you, and he asked me to make sure you understand that he deeply appreciates your valor and service to our nation and the entire world."

"Roger that!" everyone shouted to Oliver.

"See you on the ground, team!" Doc yelled as he crouched low, pulled the bag up around him and over his head with his free hand, then stood up, pulling the zipper shut as he went.

Doc's bag inflated while the other six performed the same maneuver and completed the set of seven drop bags, seven feet in diameter, and ready to roll. The dramatic moment was punctuated by a sudden silence when Harm turned off all four of the giant plane's engines for the second time, and the C130 began to glide toward the vault's exhaust ports as slowly as the pilot dared fly and just 50 feet above the ground.

Chuck watched for the green "Go" light to come on, signaling that they were over the vault's exhaust parts. When it did, he fist-bumped the button that opened the cargo bay door to the frigid -35 degree Celsius air howling like a freight train racing by.

Chuck quickly discovered that he merely had to roll the bags within six feet of the edge of the bay door before the rushing wind sucked them out into the frigid open air. The bags dropped like perfectly round boulders into the soft, four and a half feet of snow and looked like seven mammoth eggs all nested in a row, approximately 30 feet apart.

Doc was the first to emerge from his bag. He was thrilled when all of the other six team members opened theirs, giddy with the euphoria of being the first souls to successfully perform a blind 50-foot free-fall from a C130 without a parachute…and having lived through it.

"Check-in!" Doc called out to the team.

"Q here!"

"Jenny here!"

"Louis here!"

"Noah here!"

"Madeleine here!"

"Rafe here!"

"Oliver here!" came the familiar voice from the Situation Room. "Glad everyone's alright! The president's on his way down and will be monitoring the assault along with us here in the Situation Room, Doc."

"Excellent!" Doc responded simply. "Leave the bags where they lay, put on your snowshoes, and stay close," Doc commanded, and the team began the quarter-mile trek to the vault's exhaust ports. "The snow's a bit more sticky than we expected. So don't worry when you hear heavy breathing," Doc told Oliver.

"Just put the radio on 'mute' if heavy breathing gets you going, Oliver," Q quipped.

"Ignore him," Doc simply advised Oliver.

"Roger that!" Oliver replied. "It's good that you have some comic relief along, though."

"You hear that?" Q chuckled to Doc.

"President Prescott just entered the room," Oliver said quietly into the radio.

"Hello, Doc! This is President Prescott," the president's voice boomed over the radio a few moments later. "I'm glad to learn you're all alright and ready to bring our two challenges back home to us. I intend to be here until you confirm the mission is accomplished."

"Roger that, Mr. President! It's good to know you're there, sir!" Doc replied and led the team onward over the snow.

Meanwhile, deep inside the vault, Chastain was relieved when Baird finally came to the end of what the Legionnaire thought must be the longest corridor in the complex.

"Do you know what I'm about to show you, Nostradamus?" Baird asked the Frenchman.

"I have no idea," Chastain admitted.

"Get a load of this!" Baird said as he punched a large button on the wall and a door 20 feet wide and 10 feet high slid open to reveal two large vehicles.

"Woah-ho!" Chastain shouted at the sight of the two obvious solutions to the challenge of moving about the snow- and ice-covered island quickly.

"This one," Baird said as they approached the larger of the two vehicles, "looks as though it can easily carry fifty or more men through deep snow, thanks to its massive tracks. It will serve us well when we and my Guardians are ready to depart.

"This other one," Baird said as he pointed to the smaller vehicle, equipped with six massive balloon tires, approximately six feet in diameter, "no doubt moves over the snow much faster and will easily accommodate the two of us along with a driver and several Guardians."

"But how will we get them out of here?" Chastain asked.

Baird strode to the nearest wall and punched another button, which opened another large sliding door at the far end of the room, to expose a massive, long, brightly illuminated tunnel.

"That has to be the way out!" Chastain said excitedly.

"That it is!" Baird confirmed. "Carved out of more than a mile of solid rock. The door at the far end can be opened remotely by a button in the cab of either vehicle. No more snowmobile rides for us!" he said with a laugh.

The two of them spent a few more minutes climbing into the cabs of both vehicles to satisfy their curiosity. Chastain was relieved when they finally headed to their quarters. He was exhausted and could only think of sleep. When he finally returned to his office space, he collapsed onto the cot beside the desk that held the laptop, into which he earlier had inserted the jump drive, and which still displayed his scrolls.

Outside, about 50 feet above and a quarter-mile to the east of Chastain's cot, Doc and his team welcomed the warm air that engulfed them when they reached the vault's exhaust vents.

"Spread out and look for a quiet way in," Doc told his team.

"Nothing here!" each member called-out after finding no access panels.

"Well, I guess it's time to announce our arrival," Doc said and locked eyes with Louis, who had the MAHEM over his right shoulder.

"Stand by, Mr. President. Talk to you again the moment the mission's accomplished." Doc said and gave Louis the "Go!" sign.

"That you will, Doc!" the president replied and locked his eyes upon the satellite image of the Doomsday vault on the giant screen that covered an entire wall of the Situation Room.

"Time to use the earplugs Doc handed out," Louis said as he activated the MAHEM and pointed it at the center of the exhaust vents. "Stand back! Here we go!" he shouted as he pulled the trigger and launched the explosive charge

As Doc suspected would happen, several Guardians faintly heard the blast that ripped a hole seven feet in diameter in the concrete around the vents.

"Let's find Chastain, then find Baird!" Doc shouted as he led the charge into the breach.

The concussion from the explosion set off the alarm within the vault as the team raced down an incline to the innards of the ventilation room, where they encountered the first dozen Guardians and a hail of bullets. Doc, Q, and Jenny knelt and returned fire so that Louis, Noah, Madeleine, and Rafe had clear shots as they stood behind them. The team took out that first contingent with ease and move on in search of their two quarries.

Two dozen more Guardians lined both walls of the main corridor just outside the room and opened fire as Doc and his team stepped from the room.

"Time to try out the Punishers, Q!" Doc yelled as the

rest of the team covered him and Q with a barrage of cover fire from their M16s.

The pair fired the M25s and launched two charges to the default distance of 15 meters—right into the midst of the Guardians—and blew every one of them to kingdom come.

"Oh, I like these!" Q shouted with a beaming smile.

"They're gonna save us a lot of bullets!" Noah shouted.

"Find Chastain, pronto!" Doc commanded next.

Rafe sprinted into the lead as the team ran along the corridor that led to the office complex, where they knew Chastain and Baird—and more Guardians—must be lurking. The Legionnaire sprinted directly into the flurry of bullets unleashed on the team by another clot of Guardians, which made it impossible for the team to return fire for fear of hitting him.

"That crazy Frenchman's going to get himself—and us —killed!" Q shouted over the deafening gunfire that echoed off the concrete walls, floor, and ceiling.

But confused by the sight of Rafe running directly into their barrage of bullets, the Guardians slowed their fire. It was just the break the team needed to overrun the Guardians and press on toward the offices they knew must contain the men they had come so far to capture.

Doc caught up with Rafe just as the Legionnaire kicked in an office door and burst into it.

"Nothing!" Rafe yelled as he quickly scanned the empty office.

Doc quickly pivoted in the doorway, moved to the next office, and kicked the door in.

"Nothing!" he yelled to Rafe, who moved on and kicked in the door to the next office.

Luckily, that third office door swung shut behind Rafe, so Doc didn't see the flash from the Legionnaire's PHASR pistol when he fired it at Chastain, was cowering in that office under the mistaken belief that he was the meek and mild-mannered Nostradamus. Doc opened the door and found Rafe standing over Chastain, who lay unconscious on the cot.

"Mission Critical is accomplished!" Rafe said with a broad smile.

"You stay with him!" Doc said and ran out of the office to rejoin the team as they swept through the vault in search of Baird and the remaining Guardians.

Doc was surprised to feel and smell fresh, cold air as he ran down the main corridor. He followed it, and it led him to the large sliding door, where he found Q and the rest of the team in a gun battle with what was left of the Guardians who were clambering onto the vehicles Baird had discovered earlier.

"Put on your goggles, and let 'em have it with the PHASRs!" Doc yelled, and the team unleashed a flurry of flashes, with no effect. "Damn it!" Doc shouted when he realized the Guardians were all wearing the same protective goggles as the team.

He caught sight of Baird in the cabin of the wheeled vehicle as the two monster machines roared to life and began a slow roll down the mile-long tunnel that would take the murderous gang to the outside— and freedom. The team kept firing at the armored vehicles until Doc ordered them to hold their fire.

"Well, I suppose Baird and the Frenchman are both aboard, and there's no stopping them now," Q huffed as he put his Browning Mark III back in its holster. "I would have let 'em have it with the MAHEM, Doc," he said in frustration. " But the damned thing jammed on me."

"S'okay, Doc," the former SEAL assured him. "We've got Chastain, safe and sound."

"Oorah!" Louis shouted in celebration and punched the air for emphasis.

"But I can't imagine Baird abandoning Chastain so easily," Doc wondered out loud, *"unless he has the scrolls,* which is all he wanted Chastain for in the first place."

"Baird doesn't have the scrolls," Rafe said over Doc's shoulder.

"How can you be so sure?" Doc wheeled around and asked him.

"Because I have them," Rafe answered and held up the

jump drive he'd discovered in the laptop where Chastain had left it. "So all that's left is to corral Baird. Do you know where he is?"

"Yeah," Doc said and pointed to the lumbering vehicles that were approaching the exit at the far end of the escape tunnel. "He's on board that armored bucket with the balloon tires."

Rafe tossed the jump drive to Doc, knelt in a firing position, and aimed his Famas F1 at the retreating vehicle.

"What do you think you're doing?" Q asked sarcastically. "That beast is at least a mile away and armored. It's impossible to do any damage to it."

"Not for a Frenchman with the right equipment," Rafe replied with a devilish grin. "That 'beast' is a Russian Burlak," Rafe said as he focused and aimed. "It's tires are its weakest link. They are soft and overinflated to allow it to navigate through water."

Rafe exhaled slowly and fired a single shot that blew-out the six-wheeler's left rear tire.

"That's gotta be a mile away!" Q shouted. "Nice shot… but just a lucky one!"

Rafe exhaled and fired another round that blew out the other rear tire.

"Okay, so that's two lucky shots," Q said sheepishly.

"It won't stop that 30-ton behemoth, but it will slow it down," Rafe said.

"That was some impressive shooting, Rafe," Doc said. "But it looks like Baird's going to make it to the airstrip. And you can bet he's got planes in a hanger there, ready to go."

"So we're two for three," Rafe said with a smile, thrilled that Chastain was safe.

# 20

# A CHANGE OF PLANS

"**F**olks, I'd like you to meet Legionnaire 1e Classe Gabriel Chastain," Rafe said with a hand on the shoulder of his fellow Legionnaire and closest friend. "Gabriel, meet Captain John Holiday and his band of fellow warriors, one of whom is my little sister, Madeleine Marie."

"I'm happy to meet you all," Chastain said, still sounding wobbly from being blasted with Rafe's PHASR pistol.

"Let's get you back to where we found you so you can rest up before we fly out of here," Doc told him. "There'll be plenty of time for introductions once we're in the air."

"Sounds good to me!" Chastain said as he and Rafe walked with the team.

"Q, take Madeleine and Louis and liberate the folks Baird took hostage," Doc said. "They're no doubt hungrier than we are and even more ready for showers. They have a kitchen staff here, so we just may get a hot meal as well as a hot shower before our chopper arrives. Medics will be on board, so we'll airlift any whose condition warrants it. While we're waiting for them to arrive, I'll find the communication center and reconnect with the president and Oliver."

"Roger that! Omelets, here I come!" Q shouted and left with Louis and Madeleine.

Rafe returned Chastain to the office and the cot he'd found him in, then settled into the squeaky chair for a much-needed break. When Chastain fell asleep, Rafe opened the laptop and inserted the jump drive and read the scrolls his fellow Legionnaire had created while convinced he was Nostradamus. Meanwhile, Doc located a secure satellite phone in the office of the vault's director and managed to get through to Oliver in the White House Situation Room. President Prescott was on the line moments later.

"Legionnaire Chastain is safe and sound, and we have the scrolls, Mr. President," Doc said with a sinking feeling of defeat. "But I'm afraid that Baird has eluded us once again."

"Still, this is great news, Doc!" the president boomed over the radio. "Don't you worry about Baird. I'm confident you'll catch him soon enough. So focus on wrapping things up there as quickly as possible and then head back. Which brings me to an important change of plans."

"What's the change?" Doc asked as a large lump formed in his throat.

He had learned through long, hard experience that any change of plans from the Oval Office often came with a brand new "Can Of Worms."

"At President DuPris insistence, I've ordered the first chopper headed your way to bring the Legionnaire's directly to the south lawn of the White House," the president said. "I'm not any happier about this change than I believe you are. So please do me the favor of having them both ready and waiting on the runway when it arrives, which, according to the Situation Room, will occur within an hour. Believe me, Doc, the sooner I get the French and their politics out of my hair, the better it will be for all of us."

"The *FIRST* chopper, Mr. President?!" Doc asked as fireworks went off in his head.

"Yes, Doc," President Prescott explained. "I've sent a second chopper to transport you and your team. But you can relax, it's only 15 minutes behind the first one. On a more positive note, I just may have a lead on Baird before you touch down at Andrews tomorrow. Forgive me, but I must cut this short, Doc. I've got to spend the next hour on the phone delivering the happy news to the leaders of the various countries who have personnel there at the vault. Thanks again for another incredible job, Doc!" the president said sincerely and ended the call

As Doc turned off the phone, he mentally and emotionally wrestled with the change of plans, which obviously seemed inconsequential to the President. But Doc had learned early on that when it came to dealing with Baird, even the slightest change of plans could prove to be extremely consequential. So he knew he had to take it to the team immediately.

"Rafe, Q, Madeleine, Noah, Louis, Jenny: Meet me in the main corridor pronto for an update," he barked into the intercom and marched out of the office.

"There's been a change of plans," he began once everyone arrived. "Rafe, you and your fellow countryman alone will board the chopper the moment it arrives. According to the White House, it will be here in less than an hour. I saw a dozen or so snowmobiles near the vehicles Baird used to escape. So it will only take a few minutes to get the two of you down to the runway. I'll leave it to you to advise Chastain."

"Whoa, whoa, whoa," Q immediately reacted. "Please don't tell the rest of us we have to swim home."

For a moment, Doc simply stared at his friend, frustrated with his endless bad jokes.

"*The rest of us* will board a second chopper that's set to arrive just 15 minutes later," Doc finally said.

Doc was relieved when the other members of the team accepted the news quietly and returned to the tasks at hand. But Q another minute to vent.

"I knew it meant trouble when this mission didn't begin with the usual can of 'Worms,'" he said. "And I'll be damned if the biggest, smelliest can ever didn't just arrive. And it's got the stench of politics!"

"Give me a break, Q!" Doc said, unable to contain his frustration. "All we're really talking about is a 15-minute delay in our departure."

"Do you really expect me to believe that?" Q asked, knowing the answer.

"You can believe what you want, Q," Doc unloaded on his friend. "I reminded you back in Montana that everything we do can potentially involve politics. So stop your whining!"

This time, Q gave Doc a long stare before responding.

"You're right," he finally admitted. "You're right, my friend…as I can always count on you to be. Don't think for a moment that I ever have a regret about serving with you, Doc!"

"Likewise, dear friend," Doc said and put a hand on Q's strong shoulder. "Likewise."

Doc then quickly marched off to catch up with Rafe and address one final loose end.

"Rafe, hold it a minute!" Doc shouted when he caught sight of the soldier about to enter the office where Chastain still slept.

"Quoi de neuf? Uh, what's up?" Rafe chuckled at having forgotten to speak English.

Doc tried his best to sound casual, but his demeanor was unmistakable.

"You'll take Chastain and all the information he can provide back to France, of course," Doc told Rafe. "But as was initially agreed to by our respective nations, I'll take the scrolls back to Washington," he added with stone-cold seriousness and held out his left hand for the 30 seconds it took the Legionnaire to hesitantly put the jump drive into it.

Then Doc thrust out his right hand and said sincerely, "It's been an honor to serve beside you, Rafe. Madeleine is no doubt very proud of you, and you can be sure the rest of us feel the same way."

Forty-four minutes later, Rafe helped Chastain climb aboard the massive Sikorsky 53K King Stallion and moments later it vanished from sight, headed to the south horizon. At precisely the same time, President Prescott's Chief of Staff Jasper Cornwall was talking with Camilla in the waiting area just outside the Oval Office when the president arrived to officially start the day.

"Good morning, Camilla! Good morning, Jasper!" the president said in his usual cheerful voice as he paused just long enough for Jasper to hop out of the chair opposite Camilla's desk and follow him into the Oval.

"I got a call from French Ambassador LeCarre 20 minutes ago, expressing his relief and gratitude at having learned that Chastain was safe and sound. He requested a brief face-to-face later today, as soon as Lieutenant Colonel Bellarose returns. In the meantime, he asked that I thank you on behalf of France for the support you provided when it was so desperately needed.

"You know my schedule, Jasper," the president said. "Make it happen. Uh, LeCarre wouldn't agree to photos during his last visit. Ask his permission to have some taken during today's visit, for the White House media files."

"Will do, Mr. President!" Cornwall replied. "You're also set to meet briefly with Captain Baird, at 3:00 p.m. in the Map Room, as you suggested. I've arranged transportation for him, and he asked me to thank you for your quick and positive response to his request to meet with you."

"Thanks, Jasper," the president said. "Did he tell you the nature of the request?"

"He did not, sir," Cornwall answered. "But when I asked him his tone turned somber. So I suspect it may have something to do with his brother. But it's just a hunch. Will that be all for now, Mr. President?" he asked.

"It is, Jasper. Thanks again!" the president said and headed to his desk.

Cornwall glanced at his watch before exiting the Oval.

"You have a little more than 15 minutes before your press briefing in the Rose Garden. I had Camilla put the file with your background material for it there on your desk."

"How on earth do you manage so many details, Jasper?" the president asked with a smile.

"I have a great teacher, Mr. President!" Cornwall said simply as he exited the office.

When President Prescott entered the Map Room that afternoon, Augustus Baird snapped to attention. He looked every inch a Navy captain, dressed in his perfectly pressed dress blues.

"Captain Baird! At last, we meet!" the president boomed as he greeted Jonah Baird's younger brother with a broad smile and a firm handshake.

"I'm honored and humbled, Mr. President," the captain replied. "Thank you very much for such a fast and gracious response to my request to meet with you."

"The pleasure's all mine, Captain!" President Prescott assured him. "This meeting probably should have happened a while ago. Have a seat, please. What can I do for you?" he asked as he pulled a chair close to the captain's. "You know Jackie Kennedy picked out these two chairs personally. Aren't they beautiful?"

"They are," the captain agreed. "And so was she."

"She was, indeed," President Prescott said with a smile. "Almost as beautiful as Melania."

"To the point, Mr. President, I'm here to request that you do whatever you can to help my brother just as you helped me in my hour of need," the captain said with soulful eyes.

"You know I'll do everything in my power, Captain," the president said. "But why are you bringing this request to me now?"

"I suspect you know better than I that he's in serious psychological trouble, Mr. President," the captain replied.

"How much *exactly* do you know about his state of mind?" the president asked.

"I know it can't be good," the captain answered. "Because you graciously allowed me to keep my security clearance, I've learned he's spending vast amounts of money to spread chaos and destruction in many parts of the world. And I recently learned through my grapevine that he's earned 'Public Enemy Number One' status, in your Justice Department, which tells me he's probably responsible for deaths here and/or abroad."

"You've got a good grapevine, Captain," the president said and pressed him for details. "So tell me, do you have any idea what his motivation might be?"

"I can only guess," the captain sighed. "I've heard cryptic stories about his wanting to build something called a 'Forbidden Library,' and it invoked memories of how resentful he was when our father demanded that he forsake a writing career and take over the family business."

"I never knew that!" the president said. "Do you really think there might be a connection?"

"Perhaps," the captain replied. "I got that sense between the lines in an email I got from him two days ago out of the blue after not hearing a word from him in nearly three years. I feared his silence meant I had lost him. And now that I've heard from him, I fear it even more."

"What did the email say?" the president asked, choosing not to tell the captain that the Department of Homeland Security secretly monitored calls, mail, and online activity for two years following his retirement from the Navy and concluded that the Baird brothers were not communicating with one another.

"Only that he'd like to see me again soon, and that he has a date with a lady in New York this week," the captain replied.

"He told you he'll be in New York this week?" the president asked in surprise. "Did he say exactly where and when?"

The captain pulled a print-out of the message from his pocket and said. "He didn't give specifics. But believe me, he's never had a personal life, and he made it sound like it was more about business than pleasure."

"May I keep this?" the president asked.

"Of course," the captain said.

"Captain, would you please let me know if you hear from him again?" the president asked. "I'm almost as concerned as you regarding his state of mind and what he might be up to."

"I assure you I will, Mr. President," the captain replied.

"Terrific!" the president said and switched gears. "Now, how are you doing since the loss of your dear wife?"

"Okay, I guess—though I miss her dearly," the captain sighed. "Thank you for asking, Mr. President. She was a huge fan of you and the first lady."

"I would have loved to have met her," the president said. "The nation owes her quite a debt of gratitude for her fast action in alerting us to your distress so that we could quickly get you the help and medical support you needed."

"Mr. President, I'm grateful for this opportunity to personally thank you from the bottom of my heart for your fast, compassionate response to the downward spiral I was in. I only wish I could personally thank those who pulled off the impossible aboard that might warship. Thanks to them, I was present and of service to Eleanor in her last days. A lesser president may well have let the military justice system do with me as they saw fit. Instead, you compassionately saw my dilemma for what it was, and I'll never forget it."

The president sat back in his chair and gave the captain a silent, pensive look for a moment.

"This is a very rare day, Captain," the president finally said. "I have some time before the next entry on my dance card, and I can use it at my discretion. So I think I'll do that."

The president pressed a button on the intercom on the coffee table between them.

"Camilla, would you please send my chief of staff in here?" he asked the non-question.

Cornwall opened the Map Room door and stuck his head in a moment later.

"Yes, Mr. President," was all he said.

"Jasper, please go to the book and pull out the chapter about the U.S.S. Ronald Reagan," the president said simply.

"Um...the entire chapter, Mr. President?" Cornwall asked nervously.

Captain Baird glanced at the president and saw him nod his head before Cornwall gently closed the door and was gone.

"I obviously can't share everything about the mission with you, Captain," the president said. "But I believe you deserve to know a few things related to it. If you're able to read between the lines, I'm confident you'll have some idea how it was done. Besides, some of the technology that was used has since been declassified."

Cornwall reappeared in the next few minutes, handed the president a thick file, and was gone again. President Prescott shuffled through the pages and pulled several out for the captain's review one at a time.

"There must be over a thousand pages in that file, Mr. President," Captain Baird said. "Is it really just one chapter in a book?"

"Well, it's not really a book in the sense that most people think of books," the president answered. "It's an archive of highly classified information presidents have been able to draw upon since the nation began."

"The President's Book of Secrets!" Captain Baird said with a flourish.

"It's been informally given a lot of names," the president said with a smile. "Around here, it's just called 'The Book.'"

Captain Baird handed the few pages he'd been allowed to see back to the president and stood to leave.

"Did you get the information you hoped for?" the president asked.

"I did, Mr. President," the captain answered. "I had also hoped to thank them personally, but I'll certainly settle for your doing it on my behalf."

"I certainly will," the president assured him. "And

however difficult it may be to hear, I'm reminded of something one of your rescuers often tells me: Everything happens for a reason."

"I've always believed that myself, Mr. President," the captain replied as he walked with the president to the Map Room door, where Camilla was waiting to see him out.

# 21

# A DATE WITH DESTINY AND A LADY

For only the second time in the three years he'd been president, Donald Prescott awoke in the pre-dawn hours to a soft, but commanding knock on his bedroom door.

"What is it?" he asked the Secret Service agent on watch on the other side of the door.

"You're needed in the Situation Room, Mr. President," the agent said apologetically.

"Tell them I'm on my way," the resident said and quickly pulled on a pair of jeans, a western shirt Q coincidently had presented to him a couple of years earlier and the well-worn pair of western Cody James square-toed boots that somehow always made him feel more alive.

The elevator delivered him to the Situation Room seconds later, and Corporal Oliver was miraculously already there to brief him.

"The chopper with Doc and the team aboard's been hijacked, Mr. President," Oliver said.

"How?" the president demanded to know and hustled to the global map projected floor-to-ceiling on the far wall. "Where are they?"

"Frankly, the 'how' is still unclear, sir," Oliver almost mumbled. "But as you can see on the map, they're approaching our northeast coast."

"Damn it!" the president almost screamed. "This has got to be Baird's doing. I know how he pulls the strings, but how does he know which strings to pull...and when! Scramble two fighters out of Andrews! And get his brother, Captain Baird, on the phone *NOW*! And we better call French Ambassador LeCarre so he can advise Legionnaire Bellarose that Baird has Madeleine."

It took three minutes to get the captain on the phone. Ambassador LeCarre connected on a second line shortly afterward.

"Captain Baird, this is President Prescott!" the president shouted in the middle of the Situation Room. "Can you hear me clearly?"

"Very clearly, Mr. President," the captain mumbled. "But bear with me until I get the sleep out of my own voice."

"You sound fine, Captain," the president said. "I apologize for calling you at this ungodly hour, but we have a situation on our hands I believe you may be able to help us with."

"I certainly will if I can, Mr. President," the captain said more clearly this time.

"The chopper's on a heading for New York City, sir!" Oliver announced.

"Captain, I left the copy of your brother's email on the table beside my bed," the president said. "Can you tell me if anything in it might give us a clue to who the lady is he plans to see in New York?"

"I have another copy here in my hand, Mr. President," the captain said. "But there's no clue that I see."

"I know who it is!" Oliver shouted just then.

"Who? Get an address and phone number for her!" the president said, short of breath.

"The Statue of Liberty," Oliver said. "And she hangs out on Liberty Island."

"This is just insane enough to make sense," the president said in a normal tone of voice. "Baird's got a thing for iconic, historical monuments and reminders of the past. But he doesn't admire them; he destroys them! Keep those fighters at a mile radius from the statue until we know what the hell Baird is up to."

"Ambassador LeCarre, I apologize for waking you," the president called out on speakerphone, "but Legionnaire Bellarose will want to know that his sister's flight has been hijacked and we believe she's being held hostage on Liberty Island in New York Harbor by Jonah Baird, and time is of the essence."

"He's here at the embassy with me, Mr. President," the ambassador said. "We're waking him now. He will, no doubt, want to go to New York immediately."

"You bet your ass I want to go to New York!" the president heard Rafe's unmistakable French accent boom through the phone. "I can be at Joint Base Andrews in 20 minutes!"

"I'll have a fighter jet ready and waiting there to get you to Newark Liberty in another 20," the president said. "And I'll have a car there to take you to Liberty Island."

"How far is the statue from the airport?" Rafe asked anxiously.

"Two and a half miles, as the crow flies," Oliver chimed in.

"I won't need a car!" Rafe shot back. "I'll take equipment that'll get me there faster."

The president looked alternately at Oliver, the map, Cornwall, and back at Oliver.

"Do whatever you have to, Rafe!" the president shouted.

"Too late, Mr. President," Ambassador LeCarre quietly

said on the phone. "He's about to climb into the Suburban just inside the embassy gate."

"Is he carrying a phone?" the president asked.

"Of course," the ambassador answered.

"We're dialing it now, Mr. President," Oliver said.

"Rafe, can you link your phone to a headset?" the president asked hopefully.

"Already done it!" Rafe shot back.

"Great!" the president said with a sigh of relief. "Baird's brother's on the phone in case he can help us with anything. So keep this line open!"

"Jonah Baird's on the line, Mr. President," Oliver announced. "I have him muted."

"Our guess was right!" the president shouted and pounded the desk beside him. "Captain Baird, are you hearing this?"

"I am, Mr. President," the captain replied. "Guess I'm about to hear my brother's voice for the first time in years."

"Please don't say anything, Captain," the president told him. "But listen carefully in case he gives us clues to what he's up to."

"Aye aye, sir!" the captain replied.

The president signaled Oliver to take Baird off mute.

"Hello, Jonah!" the president shouted. "I'd pretend not to know why you've called, but it's pretty obvious you know what I know. So what else do you know that I need to know?"

"I've got your 'Dozen,' Mr. President," Baird said sardonically. "And I've got the precious scrolls of Nostradamus, thanks to Doc's laxity of merely stowing it in his boot. But don't take heart! Your 'Dozen' are all securely bound and about to be set like jewels in the crown of the Mother of Liberty. How fitting it is since I consider this to be my crowning achievement thus far. I look forward to stocking my Forbidden Library with the books that will be written about my destruction of this monument. It will make me and my library famous for centuries…and I'll wager that no one will ever know the names of your 'Dozen' or read that they were destroyed along with Lady Liberty!

"Now call off the dogs you have in the air, or I'll dispose of your 'Dozen' right now!" Baird screamed maniacally.

"Don't do this, Baird!" the president said forcefully. "I promise you that whatever evil satisfaction it gives you will not compare to the wrath our nation will unleash upon you in return!"

"Sorry, but the Lady and I have a date with destiny. It will take a few minutes to eradicate the dollar store security guards you keep here as window dressing. And then we'll need a few minutes more to move your 'Dozen' to the crown of the statue. So I'll hang-up for now and call you back when we're ready to talk some more about my destiny…and theirs!"

"Don't hang up, Jonah!" the president shouted futilely as the line went dead.

"Rafe, did you hear all that?" the president called out anxiously.

"I did, Mr. President," Rafe shot back. "I'll be on the ground at Andrews in less than ten minutes. I'll be knocking at the Lady's door ten minutes later."

"That's impossible with New Jersey traffic!" the president blurted out.

"Not for a Frenchman with the right equipment, if you know what I mean, Mr. President," Rafe replied with the first sound of optimism in his voice since the president first met him.

"I'm back, Mr. President," Baird's voice echoed throughout the Situation Room again. "And the last of the National Park Service flunkies you have here will be gone in just a few more minutes—*and I guarantee you they will never be back.* Then I will insert your 'Dozen' gems into the Lady's crown, and you and I can negotiate their safe return…if you are so inclined. Of course, it will cost your government dearly, I assure you."

"You know the United States doesn't negotiate for hostages, Baird," the president said.

"Then I guess I better plan to make room for the books

about Lady Liberty's destruction," Baird said nonchalantly and hung-up.

"Baird! *BAIRD!*" the president yelled on a dead line. "Rafe, tell me you heard that."

"I did, Mr. President," Rafe answered in a rock-solid, calm voice. "I'm strapping on my equipment now. I will be with the Lady in approximately ten minutes."

"I don't have to tell you how dangerous Baird and his Guardians are, Rafe," the president said. "Be careful... and shoot to kill!"

"I seriously doubt they will even see me, Mr. President," Rafe said with certainty.

"Have you got video we can patch into?" the president asked as his brain raced to make sense of what Rafe was telling him.

"I believe I do, sir," Rafe answered. "Oliver, I believe you have the necessary software."

"Working on it now!" Oliver confirmed.

Rafe set his mobile phone atop the weapons locker he brought along and situated himself in front of it while he strapped into the carbon fiber Jetwing he'd stowed in it since France.

"Ironman!" Oliver shouted when the image of Rafe hovering two feet off the runway as he warmed-up the wing's four jet-cad P400 RX engines.

He slowly spun as he hovered, revealing the pair of Baretta 92s strapped around his waist and the Accuracy International AXMC .338 Magnum sniper rifle strapped to his back.

"This is our secret, everyone," Rafe said. "This Jetwing wasn't supposed to leave France."

"I'm thankful it did!" the president shouted. "Go get 'em, Rafe!"

"Gotta' mute you, Rafe," Oliver said and signaled the president that Baird was back.

No one in the Situation Room heard the roar of the Jetwing when Rafe took off from Newark Liberty and quickly accelerated to more than 300 miles an hour, headed for the Lady.

"I can't negotiate with you, Baird...bottom line," the president cut right to the chase.

"And so I must go without them," Baird said with feigned sadness. "What a sad waste of copper and flesh and blood. I'm on my way...but I shall return to fight another day!"

"Not if I can help it!" the president shouted as Baird hung up for the final time.

Baird and a dozen Guardians rode the elevator to the base of the monument's pedestal, disabled it, and began loading two dozen 50-pound boxes of C-4 explosives into it in the predawn darkness. In that silent, deadly darkness, Doc and his team sat in chains, fully expecting to die.

"Well, Doc," Q said, unable to help himself, even in this darkest of moments. "I'd say this is the ultimate test of your belief that everything happens for a reason. Cause if it's true, I sure would appreciate living long enough to at least see the reason this is happening."

But Doc did not respond to Q's challenge in that deathly silent, pre-dawn darkness. The awkward truth was that Doc had no answer to such a stark, inescapable circumstance. He and his team were helpless within the crown atop the head of the Statue of Liberty, bound in chains and completely out of options. Or at least that's what they thought.

"I'll never call Baird by his name again," Doc said as though he would have another chance. "He definitely plays for keeps. And I'll call him the Keeper from now on."

While the Keeper and his Guardians labored more than 300 feet below, Rafe approached the Lady, flying on fumes. The flight used all eight gallons of the wing's hydrogen peroxide fuel, and the engines were softly sputtering as Rafe just managed to grasp the railing that encircled the torch in the Lady's uplifted hand and pulled himself onto the tiny maintenance platform.

"Whew!" Oliver shouted. "I thought I was going to have to look away!"

"Never fear," Rafe said confidently. "My equipment never fails me!"

Rafe unstrapped from the Jetwing, then accessed the maintenance hatch and scrambled down the winding stairs to the door that led to the crown's interior—and the president's "Dozen."

"Are you in there?" he shouted.

"You bet your ass we're in here!" Q hollered back.

"Why in the hell would Baird put a lock on this door?" Rafe shouted. "Got any idea what the four-digit code might be?"

"Not a clue!" Doc shouted back.

"Got any ideas, Captain?" the president called out to the captain, who was still on the line.

While the captain thought, his older brother, The Keeper, and his guardians climbed aboard their hijacked Sikorsky chopper and it began a slow, cautious climb dangerously close to the statue's pedestal, and prepared to fly east, into the sun as it rose over Gravesend Bay.

"Try the year the Lady was dedicated, 1886." the captain suggested.

"It worked!" Rafe shouted as he tossed the lock and bolted into the crown chamber.

Seeing no signs of a detonator, Rafe feared the Keeper

planned to trigger the explosion remotely. So he jumped to the largest of the crown's 25 windows, yanked it open, and thrust his head out. He knew he was right when he saw the Sikorski slow and begin to circle the statue about two miles away. Instinctively, Rafe shed the sniper rifle from his back, propped its stock in the open window, and worked the bolt to drop an armor-piercing .338 Lapua Magnum cartridge into the chamber. Then he turned his cap around and squinted into the telescopic sight.

Rafe's well-trained warrior mind focused intently. His only thought was to lock onto the massive Sikorsky's weakest point, just below the main rotor shaft where it exits the chopper's fuselage. Not for one instant did his mind allow itself to consider the horrifying thought that even as he took aim, the Keeper might press the remote detonator and end the story before Rafe got his shot off. But the Keeper didn't press the detonator, and Rafe's shot crippled the craft just enough to allow Rafe's second shot, which found and pierced the chopper's engine and quickly turned the massive chopper into a ball of flames before it crashed into the bay.

"You didn't happen to bring a bolt-cutter with you, did you?" Q asked to be smart.

Rafe simple smiled and pulled a mini bolt-cutter from the thigh pocket of his cargo pants.

Once all the chains were cut, Rafe hugged Madeleine tightly for a long moment, then opened the hatch to the monument's winding staircase and chuckled as he said,

"We're just 354 steps from freedom. Please watch your step, folks!"

Once again, against seemingly insurmountable odds, "the president's Dozen" returned from a mission safe, sound and successful, and perfectly happy to be uncelebrated. After long, hot showers and a fresh change of clothes at Andrews, they bounded into the familiar big, black SUVs for the short ride to the north entrance of the White House.

Of course, Connie and Marsha stood at the foot of the North Portico, waving wildly and smiling as they always did at the end of missions. But they were quickly swept inside along with the team and escorted to a small, impromptu "Welcome Back!" celebration, hosted by the president and first lady. It warmed the hearts of Doc and Q to see their wives had become so familiar and comfortable with the first lady. It was considerable consolation for the extended and perilous separation that made it possible.

But that's a story for another day. On this day, the president summarized this mission the best by saying, "One of the greatest burdens of this job is knowing so many wonderful American heroes, but not being able to share the stories of their priceless service to our nation."

The End

# EPILOGUE

When the dust settled, and the adrenalin ran its course, some important developments unfolded. Not the least of which was "the reason" Q said he "sure would appreciate living long enough to see." In appreciation for Captain Baird's role in foiling the Keeper's death plot, the president invited him to the celebration and had the team relate the short version of how they extracted the captain from the U.S.S. Ronald Reagan.

"Now I see that the reason you needed so badly to see for yourself is really quite simple," the captain said.

"How so?" Q asked, unconvinced.

"Since my first coherent day in rehab, less than a month after your team snatched me from the jaws of certain death, I'd prayed for a chance to thank you with whatever small gesture I might be able to manage. Believe me, your dilemma was an answer to my prayers!"

Back in Montana, long after the glow of the celebration had faded, the team's daily lives got back to normal. They each settled into familiar, comfortable routines. But a few fascinating developments unfolded. For starters, Madeleine returned to her musings about the missions accomplished thus far and marveled that, true to her theory, their latest mission grew her list of Grand Mysteries by three.

The first was intriguing: Since Legionnaire Chastain had never studied or even read about the real Nostradamus, what were the odds that his farewell note to President Prescott would contain the 16th-century prophet's last words: "Tomorrow I shall no longer be here.' The second stood the best chance of being answered someday: Does an unknown copy of the Nostradamus scrolls exist? The third was bone-chilling: How *exactly* did the Keeper manage to stay one step ahead of the team— long before he met the man who claimed to know the future?

Two other developments were even more positive than they were surprising:

Q began practicing for the King of 2 Miles competition. And Doc finally began working on his memoirs in earnest. Shortly after he began, he became familiar with one of the perils of chronicling his adventures. One night, just before he turned out the light, the American warrior had a thought he jotted down so that he could fall asleep without the fear of forgetting it:

*"It's the height of irony that I now hope Rafe did, in fact, secretly*

*save a digital copy of the infamous scrolls. Because the jump drive containing the original files went up in flames and deep into Gravesend Bay with the Keeper, who is finally dead…or at least it appears he is."*

*End of Book 3*

# BOOKS OF THIS SERIES IN ORDER

Find all books of this series in order here:

https://www.prestonwilliamchild.com/books

# ABOUT THE AUTHOR

I'm an South-African author of Action & Adventure novels. I've been self-publishing since 2013. I've written more than fourty novels in different series. For more information about me and my books please visit my website

http://prestonwilliamchild.com

2:19

1198

90 15 35

EASTER 20 2 II
90 15 31

34 6500

13696. 77

Made in the USA
Coppell, TX
30 March 2021